Mrs Henry Wood

Roland Yorke

A Novel: Vol.III.

Mrs Henry Wood

Roland Yorke
A Novel: Vol.III.

ISBN/EAN: 9783337031701

Printed in Europe, USA, Canada, Australia, Japan

Cover: Foto ©Andreas Hilbeck / pixelio.de

More available books at **www.hansebooks.com**

ROLAND YORKE.

A Novel.

BY MRS. HENRY WOOD,

AUTHOR OF "EAST LYNNE," "THE CHANNINGS," ETC.

" And Deering's Woods are fresh and fair,
    And with joy that is almost pain
My heart goes back to wander there,
And among the dreams of the days that were
    I find my lost youth again.
    And the strange and beautiful song,
    The groves are repeating it still :
' A boy's will is the wind's will,
And the thoughts of youth are long, long thoughts.'"
LONGFELLOW.

IN THREE VOLUMES.
VOL. III.

LONDON:
RICHARD BENTLEY, NEW BURLINGTON STREET.
1869.

CONTENTS OF VOL. III.

ROLAND YORKE.

CHAPTER XXIX.

RESTLESS WANDERINGS.

THE commotion was great. Six days had
elapsed since Arthur Channing's singular disappearance, and he had never been heard of.

Six days! In a case of this nature, six
days to anxious friends will seem almost like
six weeks. Nay, and longer. And, while on
the topic, it may be well and right to state
that these circumstances, this loss, occurred
just as written; or about to be written; and
are not a rechauffé from a dish somewhat recently served to the public in real life.

Arthur Channing arrived at the Euston
Square Station on a certain evening already
told of, and was met there by Roland Yorke.
Later, soon after eight, he went to the private
hotel in Norfolk Street, in which a room had
been engaged for him, and where he had

stayed before. Roland saw him go in : the waiter, Binns, received him, and left him in the coffee-room reading his letters. Upon the waiter's entering the room nearly half an hour subsequently, he found it empty. A small parcel and an umbrella belonging to him were there, but he himself was not. Naturally the waiter concluded that he had but stepped out temporarily. He was mistaken, however. From that moment nothing had been seen or heard of Arthur Channing.

If ever Roland Yorke went nigh to lose his mind, it was now. Strangers thought he must be a candidate for Bedlam. Totally neglecting the exigencies of the office, he went tearing about like a lunatic. From one place to another, from this spot to that, backwards and forwards and round again, strode Roland, as if his legs went on wires. His aspect was fierce, his hair wild. The main resting-posts, at which he halted by turns, were Scotland Yard, Waterloo Bridge, and the London docks. The best that Roland's dark fears could suggest was, that Arthur had been murdered. Murdered for the sake of the money he had about him, and then put quietly out of the way. Waterloo Bridge, bearing a reputation for having been a former chosen receptacle for mysterious carpet-bags, was of course pitched upon by Roland as an ill-omened element in the tragedy now. It had also just happened that a man, drowned from one of the bridges, had been found in the London docks: having drifted in, no doubt, with an entering or leaving ship. This was quite enough for Roland. Morning after morning would find him there; and St. Katharine's docks, being nearer, sometimes had him twice in the day.

Putting aside Roland's migrations, and his out-spoken fears of dark deeds, others, interested, were to the full as much alarmed as he. The facts were more than singular; they were mysterious. From the time that Arthur Channing had entered the hotel in Norfolk Street, or—to be strictly correct—from a few minutes subsequent to that, when the waiter, Binns, had left him in the coffee-room, he seemed to have disappeared. The police could make nothing of it. Mr. Galloway, who had been at once communicated with by Hamish Channing, was nearly as much assailed by fears as Roland, and sent up letters or telegrams every other hour in the day.

The first and most natural theory taken up, as to the cause of the disappearance, was this—that Arthur Channing had received some news, amidst the letters given to him, that caused him to absent himself. But for the circumstance of the letter (written by Charles Channing on board the P. and O. steamer, and posted at Marseilles) *not* having been handed to Arthur, it might have been assumed that it had contained bad news of Charles, and that Arthur had hastened away to him. As the letter was omitted to be given to him—and it was an exceedingly curious incident in the problem that it should so have fallen out—this hope could not be entertained: Charles was well; and by that time, no doubt, in Paris enjoying himself. But, even had circumstances enabled them to take up this hope, it could not have lasted long: had Arthur been called suddenly away, to Charles, or elsewhere, he would not have failed to let his friends know it.

His portmanteau remained at the hotel unsought for; with his umbrella and small parcel, containing the few articles he had bought earlier in the night; full proof that when he quitted the hotel, he had meant to return to it. Now and again, even yet, a letter would reach the hotel from some stray individual or other, whom he ought to have seen on business during his sojourn in London, and had not. The letters, like the luggage, remained unclaimed, except by Hamish.

In reply to inquiries, Mr. Galloway stated that the amount of money brought up to town by Arthur from himself, was sixty pounds; chiefly in five-pound notes. This was, of course, exclusive of what Arthur might have about him of his own. Mr. Galloway, in regard to the transmission of money, seemed to do things like nobody else: who, save himself, but would have given Arthur an order on his London bankers, Glyn and Co.? Not he. He happened to have the sixty pounds by him, and so sent it up in hard cash.

The first thing the police did, upon being summoned to the search, was to endeavour to ascertain what letters Arthur had received that night upon entering the hotel in Norfolk Street, and who they were from. The waiter said there were either four or five; he was not sure which, but thought the former. He fancied there had been five in all; and, as the one was accidentally left in the rack, it must, he felt nearly sure, have been but four he delivered over. One of them—he was positive of this—had arrived that same evening, only an hour or two before Mr. Arthur Channing. The young person who presided over the interests of a kind of office, or semi-public parlour, where inquiries were made by visitors, and whence orders were issued, was a Miss

Whiffin. She was an excessively smart lady in a rustling silk, with frizzy curls of a light tow on the top of her forehead, and a remarkable chignon behind that might have been furnished by the coiffeur of Mrs. Bede Greatorex. Miss Whiffin could not, or would not, recollect what number of letters there had been waiting for Mr. Channing. Being a supercilious young lady—or, at least, doing her best to appear one—she assumed to think it a piece of impertinence to be questioned at all. Yes, she remembered there were a small few letters waiting for Mr. Arthur Channing; foreign or English; *she* did not notice which: if Binns said it was five, no doubt it *was* five. She considered it exceedingly unreasonable of any customer, not to say ungentlemanly, to write and order a bed-room, and walk into the house and then walk out again, and never occupy it: it was a thing she neither understood nor had been accustomed to.

And that was all that could be got out of Miss Whiffin. Binns' opinion, that the number of letters given to Arthur had been four, was in a degree borne out: for that was just the number they had been able to trace as having been written to him. Three of them were notes from people in London, making appointments for Arthur to call on them the next day; the fourth (the one spoken of by Binns as having arrived just before Arthur himself), was known to be from Mr. Galloway, that gentleman having despatched it by the day-mail from Helstonleigh.

What could have taken Arthur out again? That was the point to be, if possible, solved. Unless it could be, neither the police nor anybody else had the smallest clue as to the quarter their inquiries should be directed to. Had he quitted London again (which seemed highly improbable), then the railway stations must be visited for news of him: had he but strolled out for a walk, it must be the streets.

One of the three notes mentioned came from a firm of proctors in Parliament Street. It contained these words from the senior partner, who was an old friend of Mr. Galloway's:—— "If it were convenient for you to call on me the evening of your arrival in town, I should be glad, as I wish to see you myself, and I am leaving home the following morning for a week. I shall remain at the office until nine at night, on the chance that you may come."

That Arthur, on reading the note, might have hastened out to make the call in Parliament Street, was more than probable.—He knew London fairly well, having been up on two previous occasions for Mr. Galloway.—

But Arthur never made his appearance there.
Though of course that did not prove that he
did not set out with the intention of going.
Another feasible conjecture, started by Roland
Yorke, was, that he might have forgotten
some trifling article or other amidst his previous purchases, and gone out again to get it.
Allowing that one or other of these supposi-
tions was correct, it did not explain the mystery of his subsequent disappearance.

What became of him? If, according to this
theory, he walked, or ran, up Norfolk Street
to the Strand, and turned to the right or the
left, or bore on across the road in pursuance
of his purposed way, wherever that might be,
how far did he go on that way? Where had
his steps halted? at what point had he turned
aside? How, and where, and in what manner
had he disappeared? It was in truth a strange
mystery, and none were able to answer the
questions. A thousand times a day Roland
declared he had been murdered—but that assertion was not looked upon as a satisfactory
answer.

Upon a barrel, which happened to stand,
end upwards, in a corner of an outer office at
one of the police stations, into which he had
gone dashing with dishevelled hair and agitated mien, sat Roland Yorke. Six days of

search had gone by, and this was the seventh. With every morning that rose and brought forth no news of Arthur, Roland's state of mind grew worse and worse. The police for miles round were beginning to dread him, for he bothered their lives out. The shops in the Strand could say nearly the same. When it was found beyond doubt that Arthur was really missing, Roland had gone to the shops ringing and knocking frantically, just as he had at Mrs. Jones's door, and bursting into those accessible. It happened to be evening : for a whole day was wasted in inquiring at more likely places, proctors' and solicitors' offices, Gerald's chambers, and the like : and so a great many of the shops were closed. Into all that he could get, dashed Roland, asking for news of a gentleman ; a " very handsome young fellow nearly as tall as himself, who might have gone in to buy something." Every conceivable article, displayed or not displayed for sale, did Roland's vivid imagination picture as having possibly been needed by Arthur, from " candied rock " at a sweet-stuff mart to a stomach-pump at the doctor's. Some, serving behind the counters, thought him mad ; others that he might have designs upon the till ; all threatened to give him into custody. In the excited state of

Roland's mind it was not to be expected that he could tell a quiet, coherent tale. When Hamish Channing went later, with his courteous explanation and calm bearing, though his inward anxiety was quite as great as Roland's, it was a different thing altogether, and he was received with the utmost consideration. Threats and denial availed not with Roland; day by day, as each day came round, the shops had him again. In, he was, like a man that stood head downwards and had no mind left; begging them to *try* and recall every soul who might have gone in to make purchases that night. But the shops could not help him. And, as the days went on, and nothing came of it, Roland began to lay the fault on the police.

"I never heard of such a thing," he was saying this morning as he sat tilting on the high barrel, and wiping his hot face after his run; which might have been one of twelve miles, or so, comprising Scotland Yard, and in and out of every shop in the Strand and Fleet Street, and round all the docks and back again. " Six days since he was missing, and no earthly news of him discovered yet! Not as much as a *scrap* of a clue! Where's the use of a country's having its police at all, unless they can do better than that?"

He spoke in an injured tone; one that he would have liked to make angrily passionate. Roland's only audience was a solitary stout policeman, with a prominent, buttoned-up chest and red face, who stood with his back against the side of the mantle-piece, reading a newspaper.

"We have not had no clue to work upon, you see, Mr. Yorke," replied the man, who bore the euphonious name of Spitchcock, and was, so to say, on intimate terms with Roland, through being invaded by him so often.

"No skill, you mean, Spitchcock. I know what the English police are; had cause to know it, and the mistakes they make, years ago, long before I went to Port Natal. I could almost say, without being far from the truth, that it was the pig-headed, awful bungling of one of your lot that drove me to Africa."

"How was that, sir?"

"I'm not going to tell you. Sometimes I wish I had stayed out there; I should have been nearly as well off. What with not getting on, and being picked short up by having my dearest friend murdered and flung over Waterloo Bridge—for that's what it will turn out to be—things don't look bright over here. I know this much, Spitchcock: if it had happened in Port Natal, he would have been found ere this—dead or alive."

"Yes, that must be a nice place, that must, by your description of it, sir," remarked Spitchcock with disparagement, as he turned his newspaper.

"It was nicer than this is just now, at any rate," returned Roland. "I never heard at Port Natal of a gentleman being pounced upon and murdered as he walked quietly along the public street at half-past eight o'clock in the evening. Such a villainous thing didn't happen when I was there."

"You've got to hear it of London yet, Mr. Yorke."

"Now don't *you* be pig-headed, Spitchcock. What else, do you suppose, could have happened to him? I can't say he was actually murdered in the open Strand: but I do say he must have been drawn into one of the alleys, or some other miserable place, with a pitch-plaster on his mouth, or chloroform to his nose, and there done for. Who is to know that he did not open his pocket-book in the train, coming up, and some thief caught sight of the notes, and dodged him? Come, Spitchcock?"

"He'd be safe enough in the Strand," remarked the man.

" Oh, would he, though !" fiercely rejoined Roland, panting with emotion and heat. " Who is to know, then, but he had to dive into some bad places where the thieves live to do an errand for old Galloway, perhaps pay away one of his notes—and went out at once to do it ? Do you mean to say that's unlikely ?"

" No, that's not unlikely. If he had to do anything of the sort that took him into the thieves' alleys, that's how he might have come to grief," avowed Mr. Spitchcock. " Many a one gets put out of the way during a year, and no bones is made over it."

Roland jumped up with force so startling that he nearly upset the barrel. " That's how it must have been, Spitchcock ! What can I do in it ? I never cared for any one in the world as I cared for him, and never shall. Except—except somebody else—and that's nothing to anybody."

" But this here's altogether another guess sort of thing," remonstrated Mr. Spitchcock. " Them cases don't get found out through the party not being inquired for : his friends, if he's got any, thinks he's, may be, gone off on the spree, abroad or somewhere, and never asks after him. *This* is different."

He spoke in a cool calm kind of way. It

produced no effect on Roland.   The fresh theory had been started, and that was enough. So many conjectures had been hazarded and rejected in their hopelessness during the past few days, that to catch hold of another was to Roland something like a spring of water would have been, had he come upon one during his travels in the arid deserts of Africa.   Ordering Spitchcock to propound this view to the first of his superiors that should look in, Roland went speeding on his course again to seek an interview with Hamish Channing.

Making a detour first of all down Wellington Street : for, to go by Waterloo Bridge without inquiring whether anything had " turned up," was beyond Roland.   Perhaps it was because Arthur seemed to have disappeared within the radius of what might be called its vicinity, taken in conjunction with its assumed ill-reputation—as a convenient medium over which dead cats and the like might be pitched into the safe, all-concealing river—that induced Roland Yorke to suspect the spot.   It haunted his thoughts awake, his dreams asleep.   One whole night he had sat on its parapet, watching the water below, watching the solitary passengers above.   The police had got to know him now and what he wanted ; and if they laughed at him behind his back, were civil to him before his face.

Onward pressed Roland, his head first in eagerness, his long legs skimming after. How many wayfarers and apple-stalls he had knocked over (so to say, walked through) since the search began, he would have had some difficulty to reckon up. As to bringing him to account for damages, that was simply impracticable. Before the capsized individual could understand what had happened to him, or the bewildered apple-woman so much as looked at her fallen wares, Roland was out of sight and hearing. A young shoe-black at the corner had got to think the gentleman, pressing onwards everlastingly up and down the street, never turning aside from his course, might be the Wandering Jew; and would cease brushing to gaze up at Roland whenever he passed.

Look at him now, reader. The tall, fine, well-dressed young fellow, his pale face anxious with not-attempted-to-be-concealed care, his arms swaying, the silk-lined breasts of his superfine frock-coat thrown back, as he strides on resolutely down Wellington Street! Neither to the right nor the left looks he : his eyes are cast forth over the people's heads, towards the bridge and the river that it spans,

as if staring for the information he is going to
seek.   One great feature in Roland was his
hopefulness.   Each time he started for Waterloo Bridge, or Scotland Yard, or Hamish
Channing's, or Mr. Greatorex's, or any other
place where news might possibly be awaiting
him, renewed hope was to the full as buoyant
in his heart as it had been that memorable
day when he had anchored in the beautiful
harbour off Port Natal, and gazed on the fair
shore with all its charming scenery that
seemed to Roland as a very paradise.   Bright
with hope as his heart had been then, so was
it now in the intermittent intervals.   So was
it at this moment as he bore on, down Wellington Street.

"Well," said he to the toll-keeper.   "Anything turned up?"

"Not a bit on't," responded the man.   "Nor
likely to."

Roland went through, perched himself on
the parapet, and took his fill of gazing at the
river.   Now on this side the bridge, now leaping over to that.   A steamer passed, a rowing-
boat or two; but Arthur Channing was not
in them.   Roland looked to the mud on the
sides, he threw his gaze forwards and backwards, up and down, round and about.   In
vain.   All features were very much the same

that they had been from the day of his first search : certainly, returning to him no signs of Arthur. And down went hope again, as completely as the pears had gone, earlier in the day, at a corner stall. Despair had possession of him now.

" You say that no suspicious character went on to the bridge that night, so far as you can recollect," resumed Roland in the gloomiest tone, when he had walked lingeringly back to the man at the gate. Lingeringly, because some kind of clue seemed to lie with that bridge and he was always loth to quit it. If he did not suspect Arthur might be lying buried underneath the stone pavement, it seemed something like it.

" I didn't say so," interrupted the gate-keeper, in rather a surly tone. " What I said was, as there warn't nothing suspicious chucked over that night."

" You can't tell. You might not hear."

" Well, I haven't got no time to jabber with you to-day."

" If I kept this turnstile, I should make it my business to mark all suspicious night characters that went through ; and watch them."

" Oh, would you ! And how 'ud you know which was the suspicious ones ? Come ! They don't always carry their bad marks on their backs, they don't; some on 'em don't look no different from you."

Roland bit his lips to keep down a retort. All in Arthur's interests. Upon giving the man, on a recent visit, what the latter had called " sauce," his migration on and off the bridge had been threatened with a summary stoppage. So he was careful.

" Well, I've just had a clue given me by the police. And I don't hold the smallest doubt now that he *was* put out of the way. And this is the likeliest place for him to have been brought to. I don't think it would take much skill, after he was chloroformed to death, to shoot him over, out of a Hansom cab. Brought up upon the pavement, level with the parapet, he'd go as easily over, if propelled, as I should if I jumped it."

The toll-keeper answered by a growl and some sharp words. Truth to say, he felt personally aggrieved at his bridge being subjected to these scandalizing suspicions, and resented them accordingly. Roland did not wait. He went off in search of Hamish, and ere he had left the bridge behind out of sight, hope began again to spring up within him. So buoyant is the human heart in general, and Roland's in particular. Not—let it always be understood—the hope that Arthur would be found uninjured, only some news of him that might serve to solve the mystery.

Shooting out of a Hansom cab (not dead, after the manner of a picture just drawn, but alive) came a gentleman, just as Roland was passing it. The cab had whirled round the corner of Wellington Street, probably on its way from the station, and pulled up at a shop in the Strand. It was Sir Vincent Yorke. Roland stopped ; seized his hand in his impulsive manner, and began entering upon the story of Arthur Channing's disappearance without the smallest preliminary greeting of any kind. Every moment Roland could spare from running, he spent in talking. He talked to Mrs. Jones, he talked to Henry William Ollivera, he talked to Hurst and Jenner, he would have talked to the moon. Mr. Brown had been obliged to forbid him the office, unless he could come to it to work. In his rapid, excited manner, he poured forth the story, circumstance after circumstance, in Sir Vincent's ear, that gentleman feeling slightly bewildered, and not best pleased at the unexpected arrest.

"Oh—ah—I dare say he'll turn up all right," minced Sir Vincent. "A fella's not obliged to acquaint his friends with his movements. Just got up to town ?—ah—yes—

just for a day or two. Good day. Hope
you'll find him."

"You don't understand who it is, Vincent,"
spoke Roland, resenting the want of interest;
which, to say the best of it, was but luke-
warm. "It is William Yorke's brother-in-
law, Annabel's brother, and the dearest friend
I've ever had in life. I've told you of Arthur
Channing before. He has the best and bravest
heart living; he is the truest man and gentleman the world ever produced."

"Ah—yes—good day! I'm in a hurry."

Sir Vincent made his escape into the shop.
Roland went on to Hamish Channing's office.
Hamish could not neglect his work, however
Roland might abandon his.

But Hamish would have liked to do it. In
good truth, this most unaccountable disappearance of his brother was rendering him in
a measure unfit for its duties. He might almost as well have devoted his whole time just
now to the interests of the search, for his
thoughts were with it always, and his inter-
ruptions were many. To him the police carried reports; it was on him Roland Yorke
rattled in half a dozen times in the course of
the day, upsetting all order and quiet, and
business too, by the commotion he raised. To
see Roland burst in, breath gone, hair awry,

face white, chest heaving with emotion, was nothing at all extraordinary; but Hamish did wish, as the doors swung back after Roland once more, on this morning, that he would not burst in quite so often. Perhaps Roland was a little more excited than usual, from the full belief that he had at length got hold of the right clue.

"It's all out, Hamish," he panted. "Arthur's as good as found. He went out of the hotel to do some errand for Galloway; it took him into those bad, desperate, pick-pocketing places where the police dare hardly go themselves, and that's where it must have been done."

Hamish laid down his pen. The colour deserted his face, a faintness stole over his heart.

"How has it been discovered, Roland?" he inquired, in a hushed tone.

"Spitchcock did it. You know the fellow, —red face, fat enough for two. I was with him just now; and in consequence of what he said, it's the conclusion I have come to."

Naturally, Hamish pressed for details. Upon Roland's supplying them, with accuracy as faithful as his state of mind allowed, Hamish knew not whether to be most relieved or vexed. Roland had neither wish nor thought to deceive; and his positive assertion was made only in accordance with the belief he had worked himself into. To find that the present "clue," as Roland called it, turned out to be but a supposititious one of that impulsive gentleman's mind, on a par with the theory that he entertained in regard to Waterloo Bridge, was a relief undoubtedly to Hamish; but, nevertheless, he would have preferred Roland's keeping the whole to himself.

"I wish you'd not take up these fancies, Roland," he said, as severely as his sweet nature ever allowed him to speak. "It is so useless to bring me unnecessary alarms."

"You may take my word for it that's how it will turn out to have been, Hamish."

"No. Had Mr. Galloway charged him with any commission to unsafe parts that night— or to safe ones, either—he would have written up since to tell me."

"Oh, would he, though!" cried Roland, wiping his hot brow. "You don't know Galloway as I do, Hamish. He's just likely to have given such a commission (if he had it to give) and to think no more about it. Somebody ought to go to Helstonleigh."

Hamish made no reply to this. He was busy with his papers.

"Will you go, Hamish ?"

" To Helstonleigh ? Certainly not. There is not the slightest necessity for it. I am quite certain that Mr. Galloway holds no clue that he has not imparted."

" Then, if nobody goes down, I will go," said Roland, his eyes lighting with earnestness, his cheeks flushing. " I never thought to show myself in Helstonleigh again until fortune had altered with me ; but I'd despise myself if I could let my own feelings of shame stand in old Arthur's light."

" Don't do anything of the kind," advised Hamish. " Believe me, Roland, it is altogether an ideal notion you have taken up. Your impulsive nature deceives you."

" I shall go, Hamish. I am not obliged to carry your consent with me."

"I should not give it," said Hamish, slightly laughing, but speaking in an unmistakably firm accent.

He was interrupted by a hacking cough. As Roland watched him, waiting until it should cease, watched the hectic colour it left behind it, a sudden recollection came over him of *one* who used to cough in much the same way before he died.

" I say, old fellow, you've caught cold," he said.

"No, I think not."

"I'd get rid of that cough, Hamish. It makes me think of Joe Jenkins. Don't be offended : I'm not comparing you together. He was the thinnest and poorest lamp-post going, a miserable reed in the hands of Mrs. J.; and you are bright, handsome, fastidious Hamish Channing. But you cough alike."

With the last words Roland went dashing out. When he had a purpose in view, head and heels were alike impetuous, and perhaps no earthly power, unless it had been the appearance of Arthur, could have arrested him in the end he had in view—that of starting for Helstonleigh.

CHAPTER XXX.

A NEW IDEA FOR MR. OLLIVERA.

THE Reverend Henry William Ollivera sat in his room at a late breakfast; he had been called abroad to a sick parishioner just as he was about to sit down to it at nine in the morning. With his usual abandonment of self, he hastened away, swallowing a thimbleful of coffee without milk or sugar, and carrying with him a crust of bread. It was nearly one when he came back again, having taken a morning service for a friend, and this was his real breakfast. Mrs. Jones, who cared for the comforts of the people about her in her tart way, had sent up what she called buttered eggs, a slice of ham, and a hot roll. The table-cloth was beautifully white; the coffee-pot looked as good as silver.

But, tempting as the meal really was, hungry as Mr. Ollivera might be supposed to be, he was letting it get cold before him. A

newspaper lay on the stand near, but he did
not unfold it. The strangely eager light in
his eyes was very conspicuous as he sat, seeing nothing, lost in a reverie; the fevered
hands were still. Some months had elapsed
now since his wild anxiety, to unfold the
mystery enshrouding his brother's death, had
set-in afresh, through the disclosure of Mr.
Willett; a burning, restless anxiety, that
never seemed wholly to quit his mind, by
night or by day.

But nothing had come of it. Seek as Mr.
Ollivera would, he as yet obtained no result.
An exceedingly disagreeable and curious
doubt had crossed his thoughts at times—
whence arising he scarcely knew—of one whom
he would have been very unwilling to suspect,
even though the adverse appearances were
greater than at present. And that was Alletha Rye. Perhaps what first of all struck
him as strange, was Miss Rye's ill-concealed
agitation upon any mention of the subject,
her startling change of colour, her shrinking
desire to avoid it. At the time of Mr. Willett's communication the clergyman had renewed his habit of going into Mrs. Jones's
parlour to converse upon the topic; previously
he had been letting it slip into disuse, and
then it was that the remarkable demeanour of

Miss Rye dawned gradually on his notice. At first he thought it an accident, next he decided that it was strange, afterwards he grew to introduce the topic suddenly on purpose to observe her. And what he saw was beginning to make a most unpleasant impression on him. A very slight occurrence, only the unexpected meeting of Mr. Butterby that morning, had brought the old matter all back to him. As he was hastening home from church, really wanting his breakfast, he encountered Jonas Butterby the detective. The latter said he had been in town nearly a week on business, (the reader saw him at the commencement, in conjunction with Mr. Bede Greatorex), but was returning to Helstonleigh that night or on the morrow. For a few minutes they stood conversing of the past, Butterby saying that nothing had " turned up."

" Have you not heard of Godfrey Pitman ?" suddenly asked Mr. Ollivera.

The question was put sharply : and for once the clever man was at fault. Did Mr. Ollivera mean to imply that he *had* heard of Pitman ? —that he, the clergyman, was aware that he had heard ? Or, was it but a simple question ? In the uncertainty, Mr. Butterby made a pause, evidently in some kind of doubt or hesitation, and glanced keenly at the questioner from under his eyebrows. Mr. Ollivera marked it all.

" *Have* you heard of him, then ?"

" The way that folks's thoughts get wandering !" exclaimed Butterby, with a charming air of innocence. " Pitman, says you : if I wasn't a running of my head on that other man—Willett. And *he* has got an attack of the shivers from drinking ; that's the last gazetted news of him, sir. As to that Godfrey Pitman—the less we say about him, the better, unless we could say it to some purpose. Good morning, Reverend Sir ; I've got my work cut out for me to-day."

" One moment," said Mr. Ollivera, detaining him. " I want your opinion upon a question I am going to ask. Could a woman, think you, have killed my brother ?"

Perhaps the question was so unexpected as slightly to startle even the detective. Instead of answering it, his green eyes shot out another keen glance at Mr. Ollivera, and they did not quit his face again. The latter supposed he was not understood.

" I mean, could a woman, think you, have had the physical strength and courage to fire the pistol ?"

" Do you ask me that, sir, because you suspect one ?"

" I cannot say I go so far as to *suspect* one. It has occurred to me latterly as being within the range of possibility. I wish you would answer my question, Mr. Butterby ?"

" In course, from the point you put it, it might have been a woman just as well as a man ; some women be every bit as strong, and a sight bolder," was Mr. Butterby's answer. " But I can't wait, sir, now," he added, as he turned away and said good morning once more.

" It was queer, his asking that," very softly repeated Mr. Butterby, between his lips, as he walked on at a quicker pace than usual.

Mr. Ollivera got home with his head full of this ; and, as usual under the circumstances, was letting his late breakfast grow cold before him. Mrs. Jones, entering the room on some domestic errand, gave him the information that Roland Yorke had just come in in a fine state of commotion (which was nothing unusual), saying Arthur Channing was as good as found murdered ; and that he was, in consequence, off to Helstonleigh. Before Mr. Ollivera, setting to his breakfast then with a will, could get down stairs, Roland had gone skimming out again. So the clergyman turned his steps to the house of Greatorex and Greatorex.

It could not be but that the singular and prolonged disappearance of Arthur Channing should be exciting commotion in the public mind. Though it had not been made, so to say, a public matter, at least a portion of the public knew of it. The name did not appear in the papers; but the "mysterious disappearance of a gentleman" was becoming quite a treasure to the news-compilers. Greatorex and Greatorex had taken it up warmly, as much from real, intrinsic interest in the affair itself, as that Annabel was an inmate of their house. Arthur Channing had stood, unsolicited, over John Ollivera's grave at the stealthy midnight burial service; and Mr. Greatorex did not forget it. He had offered his services at once to Hamish Channing. "We have," he said, "a wide experience of London life, and will do for you in it all that can be done." Bede, though kindly anxious, wished the matter could be set at rest, for it was costing him a clerk. Roland candidly avowed that he was no more fit for his work at present, than he would be to rule the patients in St. Luke's; and Bede privately believed this was only truth. Little Jenner was home again, and took Roland's work as well as his own.

One very singular phase of the attendant

surroundings was this—so many people appeared to be missing. The one immediately in question, Arthur Channing, was but a unit in the number. Scarcely an hour in the day passed but the police either received voluntary news of somebody's disappearance; or, through their enquiries after Arthur, gained it for themselves. If space allowed, and these volumes were the proper medium for it, a most singularly interesting account might be given of these facts, every word of which would be true.

Henry Ollivera found Mr. Greatorex in the dining-room finishing his luncheon. In point of fact it was his dinner, for he was going out of town that afternoon and would not be home until late. Bede, who rarely took luncheon, though he sometimes made a pretence of going up for it, was biting morsels off a hard biscuit, as he stood against the wall by the mantle-piece, near the handsome pier-glass that in his days of vanity he had been so fond of glancing in. Mrs. Bede Greatorex was at table; also the little girl, Jane, whose dinner it was. The board was extravagantly spread, displaying fish and fowl and other delicacies, and Mrs. Bede was solacing herself with a pint of sparkling hock, which stood at her elbow. She looked flushed; at least, as much so as a made-up face can look, and in her eyes there shone an angry light: perhaps at the non-appearance of two visitors she had expected, perhaps because she had just come from one of her violent-tempered attacks on Miss Channing. Mr. Greatorex, like his son Bede, did not appear to appreciate the good things: he was making his dinner off one plain dish and a glass of pale ale.

"You will sit down and take some, William?"

Mr. Ollivera declined; he had but just swallowed his breakfast. From the absence of Miss Channing at the table, he drew an augury that the ill news spoken of by Mrs. Jones must be correct. But Mr. Greatorex said he was not aware of anything fresh; and a smile crossed his lips upon hearing that Roland was the author of the report. Bede laughed outright.

"If you only knew how often he has come in, startling us with extraordinary tales, you'd have learnt by this time what faith to put in Roland Yorke," said Bede. "A man more sensitively nervous than he is, or ever will be, would have had brain-fever with all this talking and walking and mental excitement."

"He says, I understand, that he is going down

to Helstonleigh, to get some information from
Mr. Galloway," said the clergyman.

"Oh, is he? As good go there as stay
here, for all the work he does. He'd start
for the moon if there were a road to convey
him to it."

"I wonder you give him so much holiday,
Bede," remarked Mr. Ollivera.

"He takes it," answered Bede. "He is of
very little use at his best, but we don't choose
to discharge him, or in fact make any change
until Lord Carrick comes over, who may now
be expected shortly. I believe one thing—that
he tries to do his utmost: and Brown puts
up with him."

"Do you know," began Mr. Ollivera, in a
low, meaning tone, when the door closed upon
the luncheon-tray, and the three gentlemen
stood round the fire, Mrs. Bede having betaken
herself to a far-off window, "I have half a
mind to go to Helstonleigh myself."

"In search of Arthur Channing, William?"

"No, uncle. In quest of that other search
that has been upon my mind so long. An
idea has forced itself upon me lately that it—
might have been a woman."

"For heaven's sake drop it," exclaimed
Bede, with strange agitation. "Don't you
see Louisa?"

She could not have heard—but Bede was always thus. He had his reasons for never allowing it to be spoken of before her. One of them was this: In the days gone by, just before their marriage, Clare Joliffe, suddenly introducing the subject of Mr. Ollivera's death, when Bede was present, said to her sister in a tone between jest and earnest, that she (Louisa) had been the cause of it. Clare meant no more than that her conduct had caused him to end his life—as it was supposed he did. But Louisa, partly with passion, had gone into a state of agitation so great as to alarm Bede. Never, from that time, would he suffer it to be mentioned before her if he could guard against it.

"But, William, what do you mean about a woman?" asked Mr. Greatorex, dropping his voice to a lower key.

"Uncle Greatorex, I cannot explain myself. I must go on in my own way, until the time to speak shall come. That the clearance of the past is rapidly advancing I feel sure of. A subtle instinct whispers it to me. My dreams tell it me. Forget for the present what I said. I ought not to have spoken."

"You are visionary as usual," said Bede, sarcastically.

"I know that you always think me so,"

was the clergyman's answer, and he turned to depart.

There was a general dispersion. Only Mr. Greatorex remained in the room : and he had fallen into deep thought : when Roland Yorke, in his chronic state of excitement, dashed in. Without any ceremony he flung himself into a chair.

"Mr. Greatorex, I am nearly dead-beat. What with cutting about perpetually, and meeting depressing disappointments, and catching up horrible new fears, it's enough to wear a fellow out, sir."

Roland looked it : dead-beat. He had plenty of strength ; but it would not stand this much overtaxing. In the last six days it may be questioned if he had sat down, with the exception of coming to a temporary anchor on upright barrels or parapets of bridges ; and then he and his legs were so restless from excitement that a spectator would have thought he was afflicted with St. Vitus's Dance.

"Been taking a round this morning as usual, I suppose, Mr. Yorke," said the lawyer.

"Ever so many of them, sir. I began with the docks : I can't help thinking that if anything was done with Arthur in conjunction with a carpet-bag, he might turn up there, after drifting down. Then I walked back to Scotland Yard, then looked into a few shops and police-stations. Next I went to Waterloo Bridge, then down to Hamish Channing's, then back to Mrs. Jones's; then to Vincent Yorke's; and now I'm come here to tell you I'm going down to Helstonleigh, if you don't mind sparing me."

If you don't mind sparing me! For the use he was of to the house, it did not matter whether he went or stayed. But that Roland had improved in mind and manners, he had surely not asked it. Time was when he had gone off on a longer journey than the one to Helstonleigh and never said to his master With your leave or by your leave; but just quitted the office *impromptu*, leaving his compliments as a legacy.

"And if you please I'd like to see Miss Channing before I start, sir; to tell her what I'm doing, and to ask if she has any messages for her people."

Mr. Greatorex rang the bell. He fancied Miss Channing might be out, as she had not appeared at luncheon.

Not out, but in her bedroom. The pretty bedroom with its window-curtains of chintz and its tasty furniture. When gaiety or discord reigned below, when Mrs. Bede Greatorex's temper tried her as with a heavy cross, Annabel could come up here and find it a sure refuge. In one of the outbreaks of violence that seemed to be almost like insanity, Mrs. Bede had that morning attacked Miss Channing—and for no earthly reason. There are such tempers, there are such women in the world. Some of us know it too well.

Weeping, trembling, Annabel gained her chamber, and there sobbed out her heart. It had needed no additional grief to-day, for Arthur's strange disappearance filled it with a heavy, shrinking, terrible weight. Jane ran up to say luncheon was ready—their dinner; Annabel replied that she could not eat any. Taking the child in her arms, kissing her with many gentle kisses, she whispered a charge not to mention what had passed : if grandpapa or uncle Bede happened to remark on her absence from table, Jane might say she had a headache, and it would be perfectly true, for her head did ache sadly. It was ever thus ; even Mrs. Bede Greatorex she endeavoured to screen from condemnation. Trained to goodness ; to return good for evil whenever it was practicable ; to *bear* sweetly and patiently, Annabel Channing strove to carry out certain holy precepts in every action of her daily life. Too many of us keep them for the church and the closet. Annabel had learnt the one only way. Praying ever, as she had been taught from childhood, for the Holy Spirit spoken of by Jesus Christ to make its home in her heart, and direct and restrain her always, she certainly knew the way to Peace as well as it can be known here; and practised it. "The fruit of righteousness is sown in peace of them that make peace."

But it was hard to bear. Her nature was but human. There were times, as on this day, when she thought she could not endure it; that she must give up her situation. And that she was loth to do. Loth for more reasons than one. Putting aside these trying outbreaks, the place was desirable. She was regarded as an equal, treated as a lady, well paid: and, what weighed greatly with Annabel in her extreme conscientiousness, she was unwilling to abandon Jane Greatorex. For she was doing the child *good*: good in the highest sense of the word. Left to some governesses (conscientious ones too in a moral and scholastic point of view) Jane would grow up a selfish, careless, utterly worldly woman: Annabel was ever patiently working by gentle degrees to lead her to wish to be something better; and she had begun to see a little light breaking in on her way. For this great cause she wished to remain: it seemed to be a duty to do so.

Drawing her desk towards her, she had sat down to write to her sister Constance, William Yorke's wife. Constance was her great resource. To her, when the world's troubles were pressing heavily, Annabel poured out her sorrow—never having hinted at any particular cause, only saying the situation "had its trials"—and Constance never failed to write by return of post an answer that cheered Annabel, and helped her on her way. The very fact of writing seemed often to do her good, as on this day, and the tears had dried on her cheeks, and her face grew cheerful with hopeful resolution, as she folded the letter.

"I must balance the good I enjoy here against the trouble," she said; "that will help me to bear it better. If Jane——"

She was interrupted by the young lady in question; who came running in, followed by one of the maids.

"Miss Channing, Roland Yorke wants to see you in the dining-room."

"Roland Yorke!" repeated Annabel, dubiously. With all his lack of attention to conventionalities, Mr. Roland had never gone so far as to send up for her.

"It was Mr. Greatorex who desired me to tell you, miss," spoke up the servant, possibly thinking Miss Jane's news needed confirmation. "He rang to know whether you were at home, and then told me to come and say that Mr. Yorke wished to see you."

Annabel smoothed down the folds of her grey silk dress, and looked to see that her pretty auburn hair was tidy. She saw something else; her swollen eyes, and the vivid blushes on her cheeks.

"I'll come with you," whispered Miss Jane. "I'll tell him about Aunt Bede."

And the conviction that she might tell, in spite of all injunction against it, startled Annabel. Roland was the young lady's prime favourite, regarded by her as a big playfellow.

"You cannot come with me, Jane. Mary, be so kind as to take Miss Jane to Dalla. Say that she must remain in the nursery until I am at liberty."

Roland was alone in the dining-room when she entered it. With a delicacy that really was to be commended in one who had been to Port Natal, he would not tell her of the theory he had caught up, or why he was going to Helstonleigh; only that he was about to start for that city.

"But what are you going for, Roland?" was the very natural question that ensued.

"To see old Galloway," he replied, standing by her on the hearth-rug where Mr. Greatorex and Henry Ollivera had been standing but just before. "I think Galloway must have given—at least—that is—that he could find some clue to Arthur's movements, if he were well pumped; and I'm going to do it. Somebody ought to go; Hamish won't, and so it falls upon me."

Annabel made no answer.

"I shan't like appearing in the old place," he candidly resumed. "I said I never would until I could take a fortune with me; but one has to do lots of things in this world that go against the grain; one soon lives long enough to find that boasting turns out to be nothing but emptiness."

"Oh Roland!" she said, as the utter fallacy of the expectation struck upon her, "I fear it will be a lost journey. Had Mr. Galloway been able to furnish ever so small a clue, he would have been sure to send it without being asked."

"That's what Hamish says. But I mean

to try. I'd be off to-day to the North Pole as soon as to Helstonleigh, if I thought it would find him. And to think, Annabel, that while he was being kept out of the way by fate or ruffians, I was calling him proud! —and neglectful!—and hard-hearted! I'll never forgive myself that. If, through lack of exertion on my part, he should not be found, I might expect his ghost to come back and stand at the foot of my bed every night."

"But—Roland—you have not given up all hope?" she questioned, her clear, honest hazel eyes cast up steadily and beseechingly at his.

"Well, I don't know. Sometimes I think he's sure to turn up all right, and then down I go again into the depths of mud. Last night I dreamt he was alive and well, and I was helping him up some perpendicular steps from a boat moored under Waterloo Bridge. When I awoke I thought it was true; oh! I was so glad! Even after I remembered, it seemed a good omen. Don't be down-hearted, Annabel. Once, at Port Natal, a fellow I knew was lost for a year. His name was Crow. We never supposed but what he was dead, but he came to life again with a good crop of red whiskers, and said he'd only been travelling. I say! what's the matter with your eyes?"

The sudden question rather confused her. She answered evasively.

"You've been crying, Annabel. Now, you tell me what the grievance was. If Mrs. Bede Greatorex makes you unhappy—good gracious! and I can't help you, or take you out of here! I do not know when I shall : I don't get on at all. It's enough to make a man swear."

"Hush, Roland! I am very unhappy about Arthur."

"Why, of course you are—how came I to forget it?" he rejoined, easily satisfied as a child. "And here am I, wasting the precious time that might be spent in looking after him! Have you anything to send to Helstonleigh?"

"Only my love. My dear love to them all. You will see mamma?"

Roland suddenly took both her hands in his, and so held her before him, stooping his head a little, and speaking gently.

"Annabel, I shall have to see your mamma, and tell her——"

She did not mean that at all ; it had not so much as occurred to her. Naturally the cheeks became very vivid now. Without further ado, asking no leave, bold Roland kissed the shrinking face.

"Good-bye, Annabel.   Wish me luck."

Away he clattered, waiting for neither scolding nor answer, and was flying along the street below, before Annabel had at all recovered her equanimity.

To resolve to go to Helstonleigh was one thing, to get to it was another; and Roland Yorke, with his customary heedlessness, had not considered ways and means.   It was only when he dashed in at his lodgings that morning (as, we have heard, was related by Mrs. Jones to Mr. Ollivera), that the question struck him how he was to get there.   He had not a coin in the world.   Roland's earnings (the result of having put his shoulder to the wheel these three or four months past) had been deposited for safety with Mrs. Jones, it may be remembered, and they amounted to two sovereigns.   These had been spent in the search after Arthur.   In the first commotion of his disappearance, Roland had wildly dashed about in Hansoms; for his legs, with all their length and impatience, would not carry him from pillar to post fleet enough. He made small presents to policemen, hoping to sharpen their discovering powers; he put two advertisements in the *Times,* offering rewards for mysterious carpet-bags. But that a fortunate oversight caused him to omit appending any address, it was quite untellable the number of old bags that might have been brought him. All this had speedily melted the gold pieces. He then got Mrs. Jones to advance him (grumblingly) two more, which went the same way, and were not yet repaid. So, there he was, without money to take him to Helstonleigh, and nobody that he knew of likely to lend him any.

"I can't walk," debated he, standing stock-still in his parlour, as his penniless state occurred to him. "They'd used to call it a hundred and eleven miles in the old coaching days. It would be nothing to me if I had the time, but I can't waste that now. Hamish has set his face against my going, or I'd ask him. I wonder—I wonder whether Dick Yorke would let me have a couple of pounds?"

To "wonder," meant to do, with Roland. Out he went again on the spur of the moment, and ran all the way to Portland Place. Sir Vincent was not at home. The man said he had been there that morning on his arrival from Sunny Mead (the little Yorke homestead in Surrey), but had gone out again directly. He might be expected in at any moment, or all moments, during the day.

Roland waited. In a fine state of restless-ness, as we may be sure, for the precious time was passing. He was afraid to go to the club lest he might miss him. When one o'clock had struck, Roland thought he might do his other errand first: which was to acquaint Greatorex and Greatorex with his departure, and see Miss Channing. Therefore, he started forth again, leaving a peremptory message for Sir Vincent should he return, that he was to *wait in* for him.

And now, having seen Mr. Greatorex and Annabel, he was speeding back again to Port-land Place. All breathless, and in a commo-tion, of course; driving along as if the pave-ment belonged to him, and nobody else had any claim to it. Charging round a corner at full tilt, he charged against an inoffensive foot-passenger, quietly approaching it: who was no other than Mr. Butterby.

Roland brought himself up. It was an opportunity not to be missed. Seizing hold of the official button-hole, he poured the story of Arthur Channing's disappearance into the official ear, imploring Mr. Butterby's good services in the cause.

"Don't you think any more of the uncivil names I've called you, Butterby. You knew all the while I didn't mean anything. I've said I'd pay you out when I got the chance, and so I *will*, but it shall be in gold.   If you will only put your good services into the thing, we shall find him.   Do, now !   You won't bear malice, Butterby."

So impetuous had been the flow of eloquence, that Mr. Butterby had found no opportunity of getting a word in edgeways : he had simply looked and listened.   The loss of Arthur Channing had been as inexplicable to him as to other people.

"Arthur Channing ain't one of them sort o' blades likely to get into a mess, through going to places where drinking and what not's carried on," spoke he.

"*Of course* he is not," was Roland's indignant answer.   "Arthur Channing drink ! he'd be as likely to turn tumbler at a dancing-booth !   Look here, Butterby, you did work him harm once, but I'll never reproach you with it again as long as I live, and I've known all along you had no ill-meaning in it : but now, you find him this time, and that will be tit for tat.   Perhaps I may be rich some day, and I'll buy you a silver snuff-box set with diamonds."

"I don't take snuff," said Mr. Butterby.

But it was impossible to resist Roland's pleading, in all its simple-hearted energy.

And, to give Mr. Butterby his due, he would have been glad to do his best to find Arthur Channing.

"I can't stay in London myself," said he; "I've been here a week now on private business, and must go down to Helstonleigh to-morrow; but I'll put it special into Detective Jelf's hands. He's as 'cute an officer, young Mr. Yorke, as here and there one, and of more use in London than me."

"Bless you, Butterby!" cried hearty Roland; "tell Jelf I'll give him a snuff-box, too. And now I'm off. I won't forget you, Butterby."

Mr. Butterby thought the chances that Roland would ever have tin snuff-boxes to give away, let alone silver, were rather poor; but he was not a bad-natured man, and he detained Roland yet an instant to give him a friendly word of advice.

"There's one or two folks, in the old place, that you owe a trifle to, Mr. Yorke——"

"There's half-a-dozen," interrupted candid Roland.

"Well, sir, I'd not show myself in the town more than I could help. They are vexed at being kept out of their money, thinking some of the family might have paid it; and they might let off a bit if you went amid

’em : unless, indeed, you are taking down the money with you.”

“Taking the money with me !—why, Butterby, I’ve not got a sixpence in the world,” avowed Roland, opening his surprised eyes. “ If Dick Yorke won’t lend me a pound or so, I don’t know how on earth to get down, unless they let me have a free pass on the top of the engine.”

There was no time for more. Away he went to Portland Place, and thundered at the door, as if he had been a king. But his visit did not serve him.

Sir Vincent Yorke had entered just after Roland departed. Upon receiving the peremptory message, the baronet marvelled what it could mean, and whether all the Yorke family had been blown up, save himself. Nothing else, he thought, could justify the scapegoat Roland in desiring him, Sir Vincent, to *stay in.* To be kept waiting at home when he very particularly wanted to be out —for Sir Vincent had come to town to meet the lady he was shortly to marry, Miss Trehern—made him frightfully cross. So that when Roland re-appeared he had an angry-tempered man to deal with.

And, in good truth, had Roland announced the calamity, so pleasantly anticipated, it

would have caused Sir Vincent less surprise;
certainly less vexation. When he found he
had been decoyed into staying in for nothing
but to be asked to lend money to take
Mr. Roland careering off somewhere by rail
—he was in too great a passion to understand where—Sir Vincent exploded. Roland,
quietly braving the storm, prayed for "just a
pound," as if he were praying for his life.
Sir Vincent finally replied that he'd not lend
him a shilling if it would save him from
hanging.

So Roland was thrown on his beam ends,
and went back to Mrs. Jones's with empty
pockets, revolving ways and means in his
mind.

CHAPTER XXXI.

MR. GALLOWAY INVADED.

IT was night in the old cathedral town. The ten o'clock bell had rung, and Mr. Galloway, proctor and surrogate, at home in his residence in the Boundaries, was thinking he might prepare to go to rest. For several days he had been feeling very much out of sorts, and this evening the symptoms had culminated in what seemed a bad cold, attended with feverishness and pain in all his limbs. The old proctor was one of those people whose mind insensibly sways the body; and the mysterious disappearance of Arthur Channing was troubling him to sickness. He had caused a huge fire to be made up in his bed-room, and was seated by it, groaning; his slippered feet on a warm cushion, a railway rug enveloping his coat, and back, and shoulders; a white cotton night-cap with a hanging tassel ornamenting gracefully his head. One of his servants had just brought up a basinful of hot

4—2

gruel, holding at least a quart, and put it on
the stand by his easy chair. Mr. Galloway
was groaning at the gruel as much as with
pain, for he hated gruel like poison.

Thinking it might be less nauseous if dis-
posed of at an unbroken draught, were that
possible—or at least soonest over—Mr. Galloway caught up the basin and put it to his
lips. With a cry and a splutter, down went
the basin again. The stuff was scalding hot.
And whether Mr. Galloway's tongue, or teeth,
or temper suffered most, he would have been
puzzled to confess.

It was at this untoward moment—Mr. Galloway's face turning purple, and himself
choking and coughing—that a noise, as of
thunder, suddenly awoke the echoes of the
Boundaries. Shut up in his snug room, hearing sounds chiefly through the windows, the
startled Mr. Galloway wondered what it was,
and edged his white night-cap off one ear to
listen. He had then the satisfaction of discovering that the noise was at his own front
door. Somebody had evidently got hold of
the knocker (an appendage recently made to
the former naked panels), and was rapping
and rattling as if never intending to leave
off. And now the bell-handle was pulled in
accompaniment—as a chorus accompanies a

song—and the alarmed household were heard flying towards the door from all quarters.

"Is it the fire-engine?" groaned Mr. Galloway to himself. "I didn't hear it come up."

It appeared not to be the fire-engine. A moment or two, and Mr. Galloway was conscious of a commotion on the stairs, some visitor making his way up; his man-servant offering a feeble opposition.

"What on earth does John mean? He must be a fool—letting people come up here!" thought Mr. Galloway, apostrophising his many years' servitor. "Hark! It can never be the Dean!"

That any other living man, whether church dignitary or ordinary mortal, would venture to invade him in his private sanctum, take him by storm in his own chamber, was beyond belief. Mr. Galloway, all fluttered and fevered, hitched his white night-cap a little higher, turned his wondering face to the door, and sat listening.

"If he's neither in bed nor undressed, as you say, I can see him up here just as well as below; so don't bother, old John," were the words that caught indistinctly the disturbed invalid's ear: and somehow the voice seemed to strike some uncertain chord of memory. "I say, old John, you don't get younger," it went on ; "where's your hair gone ?   Is this the room ?—it used to be."

Without further ado, the door was flung open ; and the visitor stepped over the threshold.   The two, invader and invaded, gazed at each other.   The one saw an old man, who appeared to be shrunk in spite of his wraps, with a red face surmounted by a cotton nightcap, a flaxen curl or two peeping out above the amazed eyes, and a basin of steaming gruel : the other saw a tall, fine, well-dressed young fellow, whose face, like the voice, struck on the chords of memory.   John spoke from behind.

" It's Mr. Roland Yorke, sir.   He'd not be stayed : he would come up in spite of me."

" Goodness bless me !" exclaimed the proctor.

Putting down his hat and a small brown paper parcel that he carried, Roland advanced to Mr. Galloway, nearly turning over the stand and the gruel, which John had to rush forward and steady — and held out his hand.

" I don't know whether you'll shake it, sir, after the way we parted.   _I_ am willing."

" The way of parting was yours, Mr. Roland, not mine," was the answer.   But Mr. Galloway did shake the hand, and Roland sat down by the fire, uninvited, making himself at home, as usual.

"What's amiss, sir?" he asked, as John went away. "Got the mumps? Is that gruel? Horrid composition! I think it must have been invented for our sins. You must be uncommon ill, sir, to swallow that."

"And what in the world brings you down here at this hour, frightening quiet people out of their senses?" demanded Mr. Galloway, paying no heed to Roland's questions. "I'm sure I thought it was the parish engine."

"The train brought me," replied matter-of-fact Roland. "I had meant to get here by an earlier one, but things went cross and contrary."

"That was no reason why you should knock my door down."

"Oh, it was all my impatience : my mind's in a frightful worry," penitently acknowledged Roland. "I hope you'll forgive it, sir. I've come from London, Mr. Galloway, about this miserable business of Arthur Channing. We want to know where you sent him to?"

Mr. Galloway, his doubts as to fire-engines set at rest, had been getting cool; but the name turned him hot again. He had grown to like Arthur better than he would have cared to tell; the supposition flashed into his mind that a discovery might have been made of some untoward fate having overtaken him, and that ¸Roland's errand was to break the news.

"Is Arthur dead?" he questioned, in a low tone.

"*I* think so," answered Roland. "But he has not turned up yet, dead or alive. I'm sure it's not for the want of looking after. I've spent my time pretty well, since he was missing, between Waterloo Bridge and the East India docks."

"Then you've not come down to say he is found?"

"No : only to ask you where you sent him that night, that he may be."

When the explanation was complete, Roland discovered that he had had his journey for nothing, and would have done well to take the opinion of Hamish Channing. Every tittle of information that Mr. Galloway was able to give, he had already written to Hamish : not a thought, not a supposition, but he had imparted it in full. As to Roland's idea, that business might have carried Arthur to dishonest neighbourhoods in London, Mr. Galloway negatived it positively.

"He had none to do for me in such places, and I'm sure he'd not of his own."

Roland sat pulling at his whiskers, feeling very gloomy. In his sanguine temperament, he had been buoying himself with a hope that grew higher and higher all the way down : so that when he arrived at Mr. Galloway's he had nearly persuaded himself that—if Arthur, in person, was not there, news of him would be. Hence the loud and impatient door-summons.

" I know he is at the bottom of the Thames ! I did so hope you could throw some light on it that you might have forgotten to tell, Mr. Galloway."

" Forgotten !" returned Mr. Galloway, slightly agitated. " If I remembered my sins, young man, as well as I remember all connected with him, I might be the better for it. His disappearance has made me ill ; that's what it has done ; and I'm not sure but it will kill me. When a steady, honourable, God-fearing young man like Arthur Channing, whose heart I verily believe was as much in heaven as earth ; when such a man disappears in this mysterious manner at night in London, leaving no information of his whereabouts, and who cannot be traced or found, nothing but the worst is to be apprehended. I believe Arthur Channing to have been murdered for the sake of the large sum of money he had about him."

Mr. Galloway seized his handkerchief, and rubbed his hot face. The night-cap was pushed a little further off in the process. It was the precise view Roland had taken ; and, to have it confirmed by Mr. Galloway's, seemed to drive all hope out of him for good.

"And I never had the opportunity of atoning to him for the past, you see, Mr. Galloway ! It will stick in my memory for life, like a pill in the throat. I'd rather have been murdered myself ten times over."

"I gave my consent to his going with reluctance," said Mr. Galloway, seeming to repeat the fact for his own benefit rather than for Roland's. "What did it signify whether Charles was met in London, or not ? if he could find his way to London from Marseilles alone, surely he might find it to Helstonleigh ! Our busy time, the November audit, is approaching : but it was not that thought that swayed me against it, but an inward instinct. Arthur said he had not had a holiday for two years ; he said there was business wanting the presence of one of us in London : all true, and I yielded. And this is what has come of it !"

Mr. Galloway gave his face another rub ; the night-cap went higher and seemed to hang on only by its tassel, admitting the curls to full view. In spite of Roland's despairing state, he took advantage of the occasion.

"I say, Mr. Galloway, your hair is not as luxuriant as it was."

"It's like me, then," returned Mr. Galloway, whose mind was too much depressed to resent personal remarks. "What will become of us all without Arthur (putting out of sight for a moment the awful grief for himself) I cannot imagine. Look at his mother! He nearly supported the house: Mrs. Channing's own income is but a trifle, and Tom can't give much as yet. Look at me! What on earth I shall do without him at the office, never can be surmised!"

"My goodness!" cried modest Roland. "You'll be almost as much put to it, sir, as you were when I went off to Port Natal."

Mr. Galloway coughed. "Almost," assented he, rather satirically. "Why, Roland Yorke," he burst forth with impetuosity, "if you had been with me from then till now, and abandoned all your lazy tricks, and gone in for hard work, taking not a day's holiday or an hour's play, you could never have made yourself into half the capable and clever man that Arthur was."

"Well, you see, Mr. Galloway, my talents

don't lie so much in the sticking to a desk as in knocking about," good-humouredly avowed Roland. "But I do go in for hard work; I do indeed."

" I hear you didn't make a fortune at Port Natal, young man !"

Roland, open as ever, gave a short summary of what he did instead—starved, and did work as a labourer when he could get any to do, and drove pigs, and came back home with his coat out at elbows.

" Nobody need reproach me ; it was worse for me than for them—not but what lots of people *do*. I tried my best ; and I'm trying it still. It did me one service, Mr. Galloway —took my pride and my laziness out of me. But for the lessons of life I learnt at Port Natal, I should have continued a miserable humbug to the end, shirking work on my own score, and looking to other folks to keep me. I'm trying to do my best honestly, and to make my way. The returns are not grand yet, but such as they are I'm living on them, and they may get better. Rome was not built in a day. I went out to Port Natal to set good old Arthur right with the world ; I couldn't bring myself to publish the confession, that you know of, sir, while I stopped here. I thought to make my fortune also, a few millions, or so. I didn't do it; it was a failure altogether, but it made a better man of me."

" Glad to hear it," said Mr. Galloway.

He watched the earnest eager face, bent towards him; he noted the genuine, truthful, serious tone the words were spoken in; and the conclusion he drew was that Roland might not be making an unjustifiable boast. It seemed incredible though, taking into recollection his former experience of that gentleman.

" And when I've got on, so as to make a couple of hundred a year or so, I am going to get married, Mr. Galloway."

" In—deed !" exclaimed Mr. Galloway, staring very much. " Is the lady fixed upon ?"

" Well, yes; and I don't mind telling you, if you'll keep the secret and not repeat it up and down the town: I don't fancy she'd like it to be talked of yet. It's Annabel."

" Annabel Channing !" uttered Mr. Galloway, in dubious surprise. " Has she said she'll have you ?"

" I'm not sure that she has *said* it. She means it."

" Why she—she is one of the best and sweetest girls living; she might marry almost anybody ; she might nearly get a lord," burst forth Mr. Galloway, with a touch of his former gossiping propensity.

Roland's eyes sparkled. " So she might, sir. But she'll wait for me. And she does not expect riches, either ; but will put her shoulder to the wheel with me and be content to work and help until riches come."

Mr. Galloway gave a sniff of disbelief. He might be pardoned if he treated this in his own mind as a simple delusion on Roland's part. He liked Annabel nearly as well as he had liked Arthur ; and he looked upon Mr. Roland as a wandering knight-errant, not much likely to do any good for himself or others. Roland rose.

" I must be off," he said. " I've got my mother to see. Well, this is a pill—to find you've no clue to give me. Hamish said it would be so."

" I hear Hamish Channing is ill ?"

" He is not ill, that I know of. He looks it : a puff of wind you'd say would blow him away."

" Disappointed in his book ?"

" Well, I suppose so. It's an awful sin, though, for it to have been written down— whoever did it."

" I should call it a swindle," corrected Mr. Galloway. " A bare-faced, swindling injustice. The public ought to be put right, if there were any way of doing it."

"Did you read the book, Mr. Galloway?"

"Yes; and then I went forthwith out and bought it. And I read Gerald's."

"That *was* a beauty, wasn't it?" cried sarcastic Roland.

"Without paint," pursued Mr. Galloway, in the same strain. "It was just worth throwing on the fire leaf by leaf, that's my opinion of Gerald's book. But it got the reviews, Roland."

"And be shot to it! We can't understand the riddle up in London, sir."

"I'm sure we can't down here," emphatically repeated Mr. Galloway. "Well, good night: I'm not sorry to have seen you. When are you going back?"

"To-morrow. And I'd rather have gone a hundred miles the other way than come near Helstonleigh. I shall take care to go and see nobody here, except Mrs. Channing. If——"

"You must not speak of Arthur to Mrs. Channing," interrupted the proctor.

"Not speak of him!"

"She knows nothing of his loss: it has been kept from her. She thinks he is in Paris with Charles. In her weak state of health she would hardly stand the prolonged suspense."

"It's a good thing you told me," said Roland, heartily. "I hope I shan't let it out. Good night, sir. I must not forget this, though," he added, turning to take up the parcel. "It has got a clean shirt and collar in it."

"Where are you going to sleep?"

Roland paused. Until that moment the thought had never struck him where he was to sleep.

"I dare say they can give me a shake-down at the mother's. The hearth-rug will do: I'm not particular. I'd used to go in for a feather bed and two pillows. My goodness! what a selfish young lunatic I was!"

"If they can't, perhaps we can give you a shake-down here," said Mr. Galloway. "But don't you ring the house down if you come back."

"Thank you, sir," said Roland, gratefully. "I wonder all you old friends are so good to me."

He clattered down in a commotion, and found himself in the Boundaries. When he passed through them ten minutes before, he was bearing on too fiercely to Mr. Galloway's to take notice of a single feature. Time had been when Roland would not have cared for old memories. They came crowding upon him now: the dear life associations, the events and interests of his boyhood, like fresh green resting-places 'mid a sandy desert. The ringing out of the cathedral clock, telling the three-quarters past ten, helped the delusion. Opposite to him rose the time-honoured edifice, worn by the defacing hand of centuries. Renovation had been going on for a long while; the pinnacles were new; old buildings around, that formerly partially obscured it, had been removed, and it stood out to view as Roland had never before seen it. It was a bright night; the moon shone as clearly as it had done on that early March night which ushered in the commencing prologue of this story. It brought out the fret-work of the dear old cathedral; it lightened up the gables of the quaint houses of the Boundaries, all sizes and shapes in architecture; it glittered on the level grass enclosed by the broad gravel walks, which the stately dames of the still more stately church dignitaries once cared to pace. But where were the tall old elm-trees—through whose foliage the moon-beams ought to have glittered, but did not? Where were the rooks that used to make their home in them, wiling the poor college boys, at their

Latin and Greek hard by, with the friendly chorus of caws? Gone. Roland looked up, eyes and mouth alike opening with amazement, and marvelled. A poor apology for the trees was indeed left ; but topped and lopped to discredit. The branches, towering and spreading in their might, had been removed, and the homeless rooks driven away, wanderers.

"It's nothing but sacrilege," spoke bold Roland, when he had done staring. "For certain it'll bring nobody good luck."

He could not resist crossing the Boundaries to the little iron gate admitting to the cloisters. It would not admit him to-night : the cloister porter, successor to Mr. John Ketch of cantankerous memory, had locked it hours ago, and had the key safely hung up by his bed-side in his lodge. This was the gate through which poor Charley Channing had gone, innocently confiding, to be frightened all but to death, that memorable night in the annals of the college school. Charley, who was now a flourishing young clerk in India (at the present moment supposed to be enjoying Paris), and likely to rise to fame and fortune, health permitting. Many a time and oft, had Roland himself dashed through the gate, surplice on arm, in a white heat of fear lest he should be marked "late." How the shouts of the boys used to echo along the vaulted roofs of the cloisters! How they seemed to echo in the heart of Roland now! Times had changed. Things had changed. He had changed. A new set of boys filled the school: some of the clergy were fresh in the cathedral. The bishop, gone to his account, had been replaced by a better: a once great and good preacher, who was wont in times long gone by to fill the cathedral with his hearers of jostling crowds, had followed him. In Mr. Roland's own family, and in that of one with whom they had been very intimately associated, there were changes. George Yorke was no more; Gerald had risen to be a great man; he, Roland, had fallen, and was of no account in the world. Mr. Channing had died; Hamish was dying——

How came that last thought to steal into the mind of Roland Yorke? *He did not know.* It had never occurred to him before: why should it have done so now? Ah, he might ask himself the question, but he could not answer it. Buried in reflections of the past and present, one leading on to another, it had followed in as if consecutively, arising Roland knew not whence, and startling him to terror.   He shook himself in a sort of fright; his pulse grew quick, his face hot.

"I do think I must have been in a dream," debated Roland, "or else moonstruck. Sunny Hamish! as if the world could afford to lose him! Nobody but a donkey whose brains had been knocked out of him at Port Natal, would get such wicked fancies."

He went back at full gallop, turned the corner, and looked out for the windows of his mother's house. They were not difficult to be seen, for in every one of them shone a blaze of light. The sweet white radiance of the moon, with its beauteous softness, never to be matched by earthly invention, was quite eclipsed in the garish red of the flaming windows. Lady Augusta Yorke had an assembly —as was plain enough by the signs.

"Was ever the like bother known!" spoke Roland aloud, momentarily halting in the quiet spot. "She's got all the world and his wife there. And I didn't want a soul to know that I was at Helstonleigh!"

He took his resolution at once, ran on, and made for a small side door. A smart maid, in a flounced gown and no cap to make mention of, stood at it, flirting with a footman from one of the waiting carriages. Roland went in head foremost, saying nothing, passing swiftly through tortuous passages and up the stairs. The girl naturally took him for a robber, or some such evil character, and stood agape with wonder. But she did not want for courage, and went after him. He had made his way to what used to be his sisters' school-room in Miss Channing's time; the open door displayed a table temptingly set out with light refreshments, and nobody was in it. When the maid got there, Roland, his hat on a chair and parcel on the floor, was devouring the sandwiches.

"Why, what on earth!" she began. "My patience! who are you, sir? How dare you?"

"Who am I?" said Roland, his mouth nearly too full to answer. "You just go and fetch Lady Augusta here. Say a gentleman wants to see her. Tell her privately, mind."

The girl, in sheer amazement, did as she was bid: whispering her own comments to her mistress.

"I'd be aware of him, my lady, if I were you, please. It might be a maniac. I'm sure the way he's gobbling up the victuals don't look like nothing else."

Lady Augusta Yorke, slightly fluttered, took the precaution to draw with her her youngest son, Harry, a stalwart King's Scholar of seventeen. Advancing dubiously to the interview, she took a peep in, and saw the intruder, a great tall fellow, whose back was towards her, swallowing down big table-spoonfuls of custard. The sight aroused Lady Augusta's anger: there'd be a famine; there'd be nothing left for her hungry guests. In, she burst, something after Roland's own fashion, words of reproach on her tongue, threats of the police. Harry gazed in doubt; the maid brought up the rear.

Roland turned, full of affection, dropped the spoon into the custard-dish, and flew to embrace her.

" How are you, mother, darling? It's only me."

And the Lady Augusta Yorke, between surprise at the meeting, a little joy, and vexation on the score of her diminishing supper, was somewhat overwhelmed, and sunk into a chair in screaming hysterics.

CHAPTER XXXII.

IN THE CATHEDRAL.

The college bell was tolling for morning prayers: and the Helstonleigh College boys were coming up in groups and disappearing within the little cloister gate, with their white surplices on their arms, just as Roland Yorke had seen them in his reminiscential visions the previous night. It was the first of November: a saint's day; and a great one, as everybody knows; consequently the school had holiday, and the king's scholars attended Divine service.

Roland was amidst them, having come out after breakfast to give as he said a "look round." The morning was well on when he awoke up from the couch prepared for him at Lady Augusta's—a soft bed with charming pillows, and not a temporary shake-down on the hearth-rug. They had sat up late the previous night, after Lady Augusta's guests had left, talking of old times and new ones.

Roland freely confessed his penniless state, his present mode of living, with its shifts and drawbacks, the pound a week that Mrs. Jones made do for all, the brushing of his own clothes, the sometimes blacking of his own boots: which sent his mother into a fit of reproachful sobs. In his sanguine open-heartedness he enlarged upon the fortune that was sure to be his some time (" a few hundreds a-year and a house of his own"), and made her and his two sisters the most liberal promises on the strength of it. Caroline Yorke turned from him : he had lost caste in her eyes. Fanny, with her sweet voice and gentle smile, whispered him to work on bravely, never to fear. The two girls were essentially different. Constance Channing had done her utmost with them both : they had gone to Hazeldon with her when she became William Yorke's wife; but her patient training had borne different fruit.

Roland dashed first of all into Mr. Galloway's, to ask if he had news of Arthur. No, none, Mr. Galloway answered with a groan, and it " would surely be the death of him." As Roland left the proctor's house, he saw the college boys flocking into the cloisters, and he went with them. Renovation seemed to be going on everywhere ; beauty had succeeded dilapidations, and the old cathedral might well raise her head proudly now. But Roland did wonder when the improvements and the work would be finished ; they had been going on as long as he could remember.

But the cloisters had not moved or changed their form, and Roland lost himself in the days of the past. One of the prebendaries, a fresh one since Roland's time, was turning into the chapter-house ; Roland, positively from old associations, snatched off his hat to him. In imagination he was a king's scholar again, existing in mortal dread, when in those cloisters, of the Dean and Chapter.

" I say—you," said he, seizing hold of a big boy, who had his surplice flung across his shoulder in the most untidy and crumpled fashion possible, " show me Joe Jenkins's grave."

" Yes, sir," answered the boy, wondering what fine imperative gentleman had got amidst them, and speaking civilly, lest it might be a connection of some one of the prebendaries. " It's round on the other side."

Running along to the end of the north cloister, near to the famous grave-stone " Miserrimus," near to the spot where a ghost had once appeared to Charles Channing, he pointed to an obscure corner of the green grave-yard, which the cloisters enclosed. Many and many a time had Roland perched himself on those dilapidated old mullioned window-frames in the days gone by.

"It's there," said the boy. "Old Ketch, the cloister porter, lies on this side him."

"Oh, Ketch does, does he! I wonder whose doings *that* was! It's a shame to have placed him, a cross-grained old wretch, side by side with poor Jenkins."

"Jenkins was cross-grained too, for the matter of that," cried the boy. "He was always asking the fellows for a tip to buy baccy, and grumbling if they did not give it."

Roland stared indignantly. "Jenkins was! Why, what are you talking of? Jenkins never smoked."

"Oh, didn't he, though! Why, he died smoking; he was smoking always. Pretty well, that, for an old one of seventy-six."

"I'm not talking of old Jenkins," cried Roland. "Who wants to know about him? —what a senseless fellow you are! It's young Jenkins. Joe; who was at Galloway's."

"Oh, him! He was buried in front, not here. I can't go round to show you, sir, for time's up."

The boy took to his heels, as schoolboys only can take to them, and Roland heard him rattle up the steps of the college hall to join his comrades. Propped against the frame-work, his memory lost itself in many things ; and the minutes passed unheeded by. The procession of the king's scholars aroused him. They filed along the cloisters from the college hall, two and two, in their surplices and trenchers, his brother Harry, one of the seniors, nearly the last of them. When they had disappeared, Roland ran round to the front grave-yard. Between the cathedral gates and those leading to the palace, stood a black-robed verger, with his silver mace, awaiting the appearance of the Dean. Roland accosted the man and asked him which was Joe Jenkins's grave.

"That's it, sir," said the verger, indicating a flat stone, which was nearly buried in the grass. "You can't miss it : his name's there."

Roland went into the burial-ground, treading down the grass. Yes, there it was. "Joseph Jenkins. Aged thirty-nine." He stood looking at it for some minutes.

"If ever I get rich, Joe, poor meek old fellow, you shall have a better monument," spoke Roland aloud. "This common stone, Mrs. J.'s no doubt, shall be replaced by one of white marble, and we'll have your virtues inscribed on it."

The quarter-past ten chimed out; the bell ceased, and the swell of the organ was heard. Service had begun in the cathedral. Roland went about, reading, or trying to read, other inscriptions; he surveyed the well-remembered houses around; he shaded his hand from the sun, and looked up to take leisurely notice of the outer renovations of the cathedral. Tired of this, it suddenly occurred to him that he would go in to service; "just for old memories' sake."

In, he went; never heeding the fact that the service had commenced, and that it used not to be the custom for an intruder to enter the choir afterwards. Straight on, went he, to the choir gates, not making for either of the aisles, as a modest man would, pushed aside the purple curtain, and let himself into a stall on the decani side; to the intense indignation of the sexton, who marvelled that any living man should possess sufficient impudence for it. When Roland looked up, and had opened the large prayer-book lying before him, the chanter had come to that portion of the service, " O Lord, open Thou our lips." It was a melodious, full, pleasant voice. A thorough good chanter, decided Roland, reared to be critical in such matters; and he took a survey of him. The chanter was on the cantori side, nearly opposite to Roland; a good-looking, open-countenanced young clergyman, with brown hair, whose face seemed to strike another familiar chord on Roland's memory.

"If I don't believe it's Tom!" thought Roland.

Tom it was. But it slightly discomposed the equanimity of the Reverend Thomas Channing to find the stalwart, bold disturber, at whom everybody had stared, and the Dean himself glanced at, telegraphing him a couple of nods, in what seemed the exuberance of gratified delight. The young chanter's face turned red; he certainly did not telegraph back again.

Thus tacitly repulsed, Roland had leisure to look about him, and did so to his heart's content, while the *Venite* and the Psalms for the day were being sung. Nearly side by side with himself, at the chanting desk, but not being used for chanting to-day, he discovered his kinsman, William Yorke. And the Reverend William kept his haughty shoulder turned away; and had felt fit to faint when Roland had come bursting through the closed curtains. He, and Tom Channing, and the head-master of the school, were the three minor canons present.

Oh, how like the old days it was! The Dean in his stall; the sub-dean on the other side, and the new prebendary, whom Roland did not know. There stood the choristers at their desks; here, on the flags, extended the two facing lines of king's scholars, all in their white surplices. There was a fresh head-master in Mr. Pye's place, and Roland did not know him. The last time Roland had attended service in the cathedral—and he well remembered it—Arthur Channing took the organ. He had ceased for several years to take it now, except on some chance occasion for pleasure. Where was Arthur now? Could it be that he "was not?" What with the chilliness of the thought and the chilliness of the edifice, Roland gave a shiver.

But they are beginning the First Lesson—part of a chapter in Wisdom, William Yorke reading it. With the first sentences Arthur was brought more forcibly into Roland's mind.

"But the souls of the righteous are in the hand of God, and there shall no torment touch them. In the sight of the unwise they seemed to die : and their departure is taken for misery, and their going from us to be utter destruction : but they are in peace."

And so on to the end of the verses. Sitting

back in his stall, subdued and quiet now, all his curiosity suppressed, Roland could but think how applicable the Lesson was to Arthur. Whether living or dead, he must be at peace, for God had surely proved him and found him worthy for Himself. Roland Yorke had not learnt yet to be what Arthur was; but a feeling, it might be called a hope, stole over him then for the first time in his life that the change would come. " Annabel will help me," he thought.

When service was over, Roland greeted all he cared to greet of those who remembered him. Passing back up the aisle to join Tom Channing in the vestry (where the first thing he did was to try on the young parson's surplice and hood), he met his kinsman coming from it. Roland turned *his* shoulder now, and his cold sweeping bow, when the minor canon stopped to speak, would have done honour to a monarch. William Yorke walked on, biting his lips between amusement and vexation. As Roland and Thomas Channing were passing through the Boundaries, a rather short, red-faced, pleasant looking young man met them, and stayed to shake hands with the minor canon. It was Stephen Bywater. Roland knew him at once : his saucy face had not altered a whit. Bywater had come into no end of property in the West Indies (as Roland heard explained to him by Tom afterwards), and was now in Europe for a short sojourn.

"How's Ger?" asked Bywater, when they had spoken of Arthur and general news.

"A great man," answered Roland. "Looks over my head if he meets me in the street. I might have knocked him down before now, Bywater, but for having left my manners at Port Natal."

"Oh, that's it, is it!" cried Bywater. "Ger is Ger still, I see. Does he remember the ink-bottle?"

"What ink-bottle?"

"And the tanning of birch Pye gave him?"

Roland did not understand. The termination of that little episode of school-boy life had taken place after he quitted Helstonleigh, and it was never imparted to him. Stephen Bywater recited it with full flavour now.

"Ger's not so white himself, then," remarked Roland. "He's always throwing that bank-note of Galloway's in *my* teeth."

"Is he? I once told him he was a cur," added Bywater, quietly. "Good-bye, old fellow; we shall meet again, I hope."

Mrs. Channing was delighted to see Roland. But when he spoke to her of Annabel she burst out laughing, just as her son Hamish had done; which slightly disconcerted the would-be bridegroom. Considering that in three or four months, as he now openly confessed, he had saved up two pounds towards commencing housekeeping (and those were spent), Mrs. Channing thought the prospect for him and Annabel about as hopeless a one as she had ever heard of. Roland came to the private conclusion that he must be making the two hundred a year before speaking again. He remembered the warning Mr. Galloway had given him in regard to Arthur, and got away in safety.

Home again then to Lady Augusta's, where he stayed till past mid-day, and then started for the station to take the train for London. Fearing there might be a procession to escort him off, the old family barouche ordered out, or something of that, for Roland remembered his mother of old, he stole a march on them and got out alone, his brown paper parcel in his hand and three or four smaller ones, containing toys and cakes that Fanny was sending to Gerald's children. His intention had been to dash through the streets at speed, remembering Mr. Butterby's friendly caution. But the once well-known spots had charms for Roland, and he halted to gaze at nearly every step. The Guildhall, the market-house, the churches : all the old familiar places that had grown to his memory when far away from them. Before Mrs. Jenkins's house he came to a full stop : not the one in which Mr. Ollivera had met his death, but the smaller dwelling beside it. From the opposite side of the way stood Roland, while he gazed. The shop sold a different kind of wares now; but Roland had no difficulty in recognising it. In the parlour behind he had revelled in the luxurious tea and toasted muffins; in that top room, whose windows faced him, poor humble Jenkins had died. Away on at last up the street, he and his parcels, looking to the right and the left. Once upon a time, the Lady Augusta Yorke, seduced by certain golden visions imparted to her by Roland, had gone to bed and dreamt of driving about a charming city whose streets were paved with malachite marble, all brilliant to glance upon ; many a time and oft had poor Roland dreamt of the charms of these Helstonleigh streets when he was fighting a fight with starvation at Port Natal. Looking upon them now, he rubbed his eyes in doubt and wonder. Could *these* be the fine wide streets of the former days? They seemed to have contracted to a narrow width, to be mean and shabby.

The houses appeared poor, the very Guildhall itself small. Ah me! The brightness had worn off the gold.

Roland walked on with the slow step of disappointment, scanning the faces he met. He knew none. Eight years had passed since his absence, and the place and the people were changed to him. Involuntarily the words of that ever-beautiful song, that most of us know by heart, came surging up in his memory, as he gazed wistfully from side to side.

> "Strange to me now are the forms I meet
> When I visit the dear old town."

Strange enough. Was it for this, he had come back? Often and often during his wanderings in the far-away African land, had other lines of the same sweet song beaten their refrain in his brain when yearning for Helstonleigh. There was a certain amount of sentiment in Roland Yorke, for all his straight-forward practicability.

> "Often I think of the beautiful town
>   That is seated by the sea;
> Often in thought go up and down
> The pleasant streets of that dear old town,
>   And my youth comes back to me.
>   And a verse of a Lapland song
>   Is haunting my memory still:
>   A boy's will is the wind's will,
> And the thoughts of youth are long, long thoughts.

"I can see the shadowy lines of its trees,
　　And catch in sudden gleams
The sheen of the far-surrounding seas
And islands that were the Hesperides
　　Of all my boyish dreams.
　　　　And the burden of that old song,
　　　　It murmurs and whispers still:
　　　　A boy's will is the wind's will,
And the thoughts of youth are long, long thoughts."

There were no seas around Helstonleigh, but the resemblance was near enough for Roland, as it has been for others. Other verses of the song seemed to be strangely realized to him now, as he walked along.

"There are things of which I may not speak;
　　There are dreams that cannot die;
There are thoughts that make the strong heart weak
And bring a pallor into the cheek,
　　And a mist before the eye.
　　　　And the words of that fatal song
　　　　Come over me like a chill:
　　　　A boy's will is the wind's will,
And the thoughts of youth are long, long thoughts.

"I can see the breezy dome of groves,
　　The shadows of Deering's woods;
And the friendships old and the early loves
Come back with the Sabbath sound, as of doves
　　In quiet neighbourhoods.
　　　　And the verse of that sweet old song,
　　　　It flutters and murmurs still;
　　　　A boy's will is the wind's will,
And the thoughts of youth are long, long thoughts.

" And Deering's woods are fresh and fair,
    And with joy that is almost pain
My heart goes back to wander there ;
And among the dreams of the days that were
    I find my lost youth again.
        And the strange and beautiful song,
        The groves are repeating it still :
        A boy's will is the wind's will,
And the thoughts of youth are long, long thoughts."

Believe it or not as you will, of practical, matter-of-fact Roland, these oft-quoted lines (but never too often) told their refrain in his brain as he paced the streets of Helstonleigh, just as they had done in exile.

He went round by Hazledon ; and William Yorke came forward in the hall to meet him, with out-stretched hand.

" I knew you would not leave without coming in."

" It's to see Constance, not you," answered Roland.

Constance was ready for him ; the same sweet woman Roland in his earlier days had thought the perfection of all that was fair and excellent. He thought her so still. She had her children brought down, and took the baby in her arms. Roland made them brilliant offerings in prospective, in the shape of dolls and rocking-horses : and whispered to their mother his romance about Annabel. She wished him luck, laughing all the while.

" When William was in London this summer he thought Hamish was looking a little thin," said Constance. " Is he well ?"

" Oh, he's well enough," answered Roland. But his face flushed a dusky red as he spoke, for the question recalled the strange idea that had flashed into his mind, unbidden, the past night ; and Mr. Roland thought himself guilty for it, and resented it accordingly. " You never saw such a lovely little fairy as Nelly is."

But he had no time to stay. Roland went out on the run ; and just fell into the arms of a certain Mr. Simms : one of the few individuals he had particularly hoped to avoid.

Mr. Simms knew him. That it was a Yorke there could be no doubt ; and a minute's pause sufficed to show him that it was no other than the truant Roland. Civilly, but firmly, Mr. Simms arrested progress.

" Is it you, Mr. Roland Yorke ?"

" Yes, it's me," said Roland. " I'm only at Helstonleigh for a few hours and was in hopes of getting off again without meeting any of you," he candidly added. " You're fit to swear at me, I suppose, Simms, for never having sent you the money ?"

" I certainly expected to be paid long before this, Mr. Yorke."

" So did I," said Roland. " I'd have sent it you had I been able. I would, Simms ; honour bright. How much is it ? Five pounds ?"

" And seven shillings added on to it."

" Ay. I've got the list somewhere. It's over forty pounds that I owe in the place altogether, getting on for fifty : and every soul of you shall be paid with interest as soon as I can scrape the money together. I've had nothing but ill-luck since I left here, Simms, and it has not turned yet."

" It was said you went to foreign parts to make your fortune, sir. My lady herself told me you were safe to come home with one."

" And I thought I was," gloomily answered Roland. " Instead of that, Simms, I got home without a shirt to my back. I've gone in for work this many a year now, but somehow fortune's not with me. I work daily, every bit as hard and long as you do, Simms ; perhaps harder ; and I can hardly keep myself. I've not been able to do a stroke since this dreadful business about Arthur Channing —which brought me down here."

" Is he found, sir ? We shouldn't like to lose such a one as him."

" He's neither found nor likely to be," said Roland, shaking his head. " Old Galloway declares it will be his death : I'm not sure but it'll be mine. And now I must be off, Simms, and I leave you my honest word that I'll send you the money as soon as ever it is in my power. I'd like to pay you all with interest. You shall be the first of them to get it."

" I suppose you couldn't pay me a trifle off it now, Mr. Yorke ? A pound or so."

" Bless your heart !" cried Roland, in wide astonishment. " A pound or so ! I don't possess it. I pawned my black dress-suit for thirty shillings to come down upon, and travelled third class. Good-bye, old Simms ; I shall lose the train."

He went off like a shot. Mr. Simms, looking after the well-dressed gentleman, did not know what to make of the plea of poverty.

Roland went whirling back to London again, third class, and arrived at the Paddington terminus in a fever. That the worst had happened to Arthur, whatever that worst might be, he no longer entertained a shadow of doubt. His thirty shillings (we might never have known he had been so rich but for the candid avowal to Mr. Simms) were not quite exhausted, and Roland put his parcels into a hansom and drove down to Mrs. Gerald Yorke's.

To find that lady in tears was nothing unusual; the rule, in fact, rather than the exception; she was seated on the floor by the firelight in the evening's approaching dusk, and the three little girls with her. The grief was not much more than usual. Gerald had been at home, and in a fit of bitter anger had absolutely forbidden her to take the children to drink tea with little Nelly Channing at four o'clock, as invited. Four o'clock had struck; five too; and the disappointed mother and children had cried through the hour.

"It is too bad of Gerald," cried sympathising Roland, putting his parcels on the table.

"Yes it *is*; not to let us go *there*," sobbed Mrs. Yorke. "All Gerald's money is gone, too, and he went off without answering me when I said I must have some. I don't possess as much as a fourpenny-piece in the world; and we've not got an atom of tea or butter in the house and can have no tea at home, and we've only one scuttle of coals left, for I've just rung for some and the girl says so, and—oh, I wish I was dead!"

Roland felt in his pockets, and found three

shillings and twopence. It was all *he* possessed. This he put on the table, wishing it was fifty times as much. His heart was good to help all the world.

"I'm ashamed of its being such a trifle," said he, pulling at his whiskers in mortification. "If I were rich I'd be glad to help everybody. Perhaps it'll buy a quarter of butter and a bit of tea, and half a hundred of coals."

"And for him to deny our going there!" repeated Winny, getting up to take the money, and then rocking herself violently. "You know the state we were in all the summer: Gerald next door to penniless and going about in fear of the bum-bailies," she continued, adhering in moments of agitation to her provincial expressions. "We wanted everything; rent, and clothes, and food; and if it had not been for a friend who continually helped us we might just have starved."

"It was your mother," said Roland.

"But it was not my mother," answered Mrs. Yorke, ceasing her rocking to lean forward, and her cheeks and eyes looked alike bright in the flashing firelight. "It was Mr. Channing."

"What?"

She could not be reticent, and explained all.

How Hamish, or his wife for him, had helped them, even to the paying of boot-bills for Gerald. Roland sat amazed. Things that had somewhat puzzled even his careless nature were becoming clear.

"And did Gerald not know of this?"

"As if I should dare to tell him! He thinks it all comes from my mother. Oh, Roland, you don't know how good and kind Hamish Channing is! he is more like one of Heaven's angels. I think, I do really think, I must have died, or come to a bad end, but for him. He is the least selfish man I ever knew in the world; the most thoughtful and generous."

"*I* know what Hamish is," assented Roland, with energy. "And to think that he has got to bear all this awful sorrow about his best brother—Arthur!"

"Oh, Arthur is found. He is all right," said Mrs. Yorke, quietly.

"What!" shouted Roland, starting from his chair.

"Arthur has been at Marseilles all the while. Hamish had a letter from him this morning."

A prolonged stare; a rubbing of the amazed face that had turned to a white heat; and Roland caught up his hat, and went out with a bang. Half a moment, and he was back again, sweeping his parcels from the table to the children on the carpet.

" It's cakes and toys from Fanny," said he. " Go into them, you chickens. That other's a shirt, Mrs. Yorke : I can't stay for it now."

On the stairs, as he was leaping down, Roland unfortunately encountered the servant maid carrying up a scuttle of coals. It was not a moment to consider maids and scuttles. Down went the coals, down went the maid. Roland took a flying leap over the *débris*, and was half way on his road to Hamish Channing's before the bewildered landlady, arriving on the scene, could understand what the matter was.

The explanation of what had been a most unpleasant mystery was so very simple and natural, that the past fright and apprehension seemed almost like a take-in. It shall be given at once ; though the reader will readily understand that at present Hamish knew nothing of the details, only the bare fact that Arthur was alive and well. He would have to wait for them until Arthur's return.

Amidst the letters handed to Arthur Channing by the waiter of the hotel that night in Norfolk Street, was one from Marseilles, stating that Charles, just before landing, had

had a relapse, and was lying at Marseilles dangerously ill—his life despaired of. Perhaps in the flurry of the moment, Arthur did not and could not act so reasonably as he might have done. All his thoughts ran on the question—How could he in the shortest space of time get to Marseilles? By dint of starting on the instant—on the instant, mind—and taking a fleet cab, he might get to London Bridge in time to catch the Dover mail-train. Taking up his hat and letters, he ran out of the coffee-room calling aloud for the waiter. Nobody responded: nobody, as it would appear, was at that moment in the way to hear him. Afraid of even an instant's detention, he did not wait, but ran out of the hotel, up Norfolk Street, hailed a passing hansom, and reached London Bridge Station before the train started. From Dover to Calais the boat had an exceedingly calm passage, and Arthur was enabled to write some short notes in the cabin, getting ink and paper from the steward: one to the hotel that he had, as may be said, surreptitiously quitted, one to Hamish, one to Roland, one to Mr. Galloway, one to Mr. Galloway's London agents. Arthur, always considerate, ever willing to spare others anxiety and pain, did not say *why* he was hastening to Marseilles, but merely stated that he had determined on proceeding thither, instead of awaiting Charles in London. These letters he gave to a French commissionaire on landing in Calais, with money to buy the necessary stamps, and a gratuity to himself; ordering him to post them as soon as might be. Whether the man quietly pocketed the money and suppressed the letters, or whether he had in his turn entrusted them to some one else to post, who lost or forgot them, would never be ascertained. Arthur, all unconscious of the commotion he was causing at home, arrived quietly at Marseilles, and there found Charles very ill, not quite out of danger. For some days he was wholly occupied with him, and did not write at all : as he had said nothing about the illness, he knew there could be no anxiety. Now that he did write, Charles was getting better rapidly. It may just be observed, that the letter left in the rack of the hotel (that came on with the rest of the steamer's letters from Marseilles) had served to complicate matters ; but for that letter it would have been surmised that Arthur had received unfavourable news of Charles, and had gone on to him. The accident was indeed a singular one, which left *that* letter in the rack : and even the thought that there should have been a second from Marseilles never occurred to them. All these, and other details, Hamish Channing would have to wait for. He could afford to do so—holding that new letter of relief in his hand, which stated that Charles was eager to continue his journey homewards, so that they should probably be in London soon after its receipt.

"Oh, Hamish, it is good!" cried Roland, who had sat listening with all his heart and eyes. "It's like a great bright star come down from Heaven. It's like a gala-day."

"I dare say there is a letter waiting for you at Mrs. J.'s, friend."

"Of course there is," decided Roland. "As if Arthur would forget me! Old Galloway won't die yet."

But, even in that short absence of a day and a night, Roland seemed to see that Hamish Channing's face had grown thinner: the fine skin more transparent, the genial blue eyes brighter.

CHAPTER XXXIII.

A STARTLING AVOWAL.

Cuff Court, Fleet Street; and a frosty day
in December. The year has gone on some six
or seven weeks since the last chapter, and
people are beginning to talk of the rapidly-
advancing Christmas.

Over the fire, in the little room in Cuff
Court, where you once saw him by gas-light,
sits Mr. Butterby. The room is bright enough
with sunlight now; the sunlight of the cold,
clear day; a great deal brighter than Mr.
Butterby himself, who is dull as ditch-water,
and in a sulky temper.

"I've been played with; that's what I've
been," says Butterby in soliloquy. "Bede
Greatorex bothers me to be still, to be passive; and when I keep still and passive, and
stop down at Helstonleigh, taking no steps,
saying nothing to living mortal, letting the
thing die away, if it will die, *he* makes a mu'l
of it up here in town. Why couldn't he

have kept his father and Parson Ollivera
quiet? Never a lawyer going, but must be
sharp enough for that. Not he. He does
nothing of the sort, but lets one or both of
'em work, and ferret, and worry, and discover
that Godfrey Pitman has turned up, and find
out that *I* knew of it, and go to head-quarters and report me for negligence! I get a
curt telegram to come to town, and here's the
deuce to pay!"

Mr. Butterby turned round, snatched up a
few papers that lay on the table, glanced over
the writing, and resumed his soliloquy when
he had put them down again.

"Jelf has it in hand here, and I've not yet
got to see him. Not of much use my seeing
him before I've heard what Bede Greatorex
has to say. One thing they've not been sharp
enough to discover yet—*where Godfrey Pitman is to be found.* Foster in Birmingham
holds his tongue, Johnson shows Jelf the door
when he goes to ask about Winter: and there
they are, Jelf and the Parson, or Jelf and
Mr. Greatorex—whichever of them two it is
that's stirring—mooning up and down England after Pitman, little thinking he's close at
home, right under their very noses. I and
Bede Greatorex hold *that* secret tight; but I
don't think I shall feel inclined to hold it

long. 'Where *is* Pitman?' says the sergeant to me yesterday, at head-quarters. 'Ah!' says I, 'that's just the problem we are some of us trying to work out.'"

Mr. Butterby stopped, cracked the coal fiercely, which sent up a blaze of sparks, and waited. Resuming after a while.

"And it *is* a problem; one *I* can't make come square just yet. There's Brown—as good call him by one alias as another—keeping as quiet as a mouse, knowing that he is being looked after for the murder of Counsellor Ollivera. What's his motive in keeping dark? The debts he left behind him in Birmingham are paid; Johnson and Teague acknowledge his innocence in that past transaction of young Master Samuel's; they are, so to say, his friends, and the man knows all this. Why, then, don't he come forward and reap the benefit of the acquittal, and put himself clear before the world, and say— Neither am I guilty of the other thing—the counsellor's death? Of course, when Jelf and Jelf's masters know he is hiding himself somewhere, and does *not* come forward, they assume that he dare not, that he was the man who did it. I'd not swear but he was, either. Looking at it in a broad point of view, one can't help seeing that he must have some urgent motive for his silence—and what that motive is, one may give a shrewd guess at: that he is screening himself or somebody else. There's only one other in the world that he would screen, I expect, and that's Alletha Rye."

A long pause. A pause of silence. Mr. Butterby's face, with all his professional craft, had as puzzled a look on it as any ordinary mortal's might wear.

" I suspected Alletha Rye more than anybody at the time. Don't suspect her now. Don't *think* it was her; wouldn't swear it wasn't, though. And, in spite of your injunction to be still, Mr. Bede Greatorex, I'll go into the thing a bit for my own satisfaction."

Looking over the papers on the table again, he locked them up, and sat down to write a letter or two. Somebody then came in to see him on business—which business does not concern us. And so time passed on, and when the sunlight had faded into dusk, Mr. Butterby put on a top pilot-coat of rough blue cloth, and went out. The shops were lighted, displaying their attractions for the advancing Christmas, and Mr. Butterby had leisure to glance at them with critical approval as he passed.

These past few weeks had not brought

forth much to tell of in regard to general matters. Arthur and Charles Channing had passed through London on their way to Helstonleigh; Roland Yorke had resumed his daily and evening work, and had moreover given his confidence to Sir Vincent Yorke (nothing daunted by that gentleman's previous repulse) on the subject of Annabel Channing, and in his sanguine temperament was looking ever for the place Vincent was to get him; and James Channing drew nearer and nearer to another world. But this world was slow to perceive it—Hamish, the bright! Three or four times a week Roland snatched a minute to dart down to the second-hand furniture shops in Tottenham Court Road, there to inquire prices, and lay in a stock of practical information as to the number and nature of articles, useful and ornamental, indispensable for a gentleman and lady going into housekeeping.

But Mr. Butterby was on his way to Mrs. Jones's residence, and we must follow him. Halting opposite the house to take a survey of it, he saw that there was no light in Mr. Ollivera's sitting-room: there was no light anywhere, that he could see. By which fact he gathered that the clergyman was not at home: and that was satisfactory, as he did not much care to come in contact with him just at the present uncertain state of affairs.

Crossing the street, he knocked gently at the door. Miss Rye answered it, nobody but herself being in the house. A street gas-lamp shone full on her face, and the start she gave was quite visible to Mr. Butterby. He walked straight in to Mrs. Jones's parlour, saying he had come to see her; her, Alletha Rye. Her work lay on the red table-cover by the lamp; Mr. Butterby sat down in the shade and threw back his coat; she stood by the fire and nervously stirred it, her hands trembling, her face blanching.

"When that there unhappy event took place at Helstonleigh, the death of Counsellor Ollivera, now getting on for five years back, there was a good deal of doubt encompassing it round about, Miss Rye," he suddenly began.

"Doubt?" she rejoined, faintly, sitting down to the table and catching up her work.

"Yes, doubt. I mean as to how the death was caused. Some said it was a murder, and some said it was his own doing—suicide."

"Everybody said it was a suicide!" she interrupted, with trembling eagerness, her shaking fingers plying the needle as if she

were working for very life. "The coroner
and jury decided it to be one."

"Not quite everybody," dissented Mr. Butterby, listening with composure until she had
finished. "*You* didn't. I was in the church-
yard when they put him into the ground, and
heard and saw you over the grave."

"But I had cause to—to—alter my opinion,
later," she said, her face turning hectic with
emotion. "Heaven alone knows how bitterly
I have repented of that night's work! If cutting my tongue out afterwards, instead of before, could have undone my mistake——"

"Now look here; don't you get flurried,"
interposed Mr. Butterby. "I didn't come
here to put you out, but just to have a
rational talk on a point or two. I thought at
the time it was a suicide, as you may remember: but I'm free to confess that the way
in which the ball has been kept rolling since
has served to alter my opinion. Counsellor
Ollivera was murdered!"

She made no reply. Taking up her scis-
sors, she began cutting away at the work at
random, and the hectic red faded to a sickly
whiteness.

"There was a stranger lodging at Mrs.
Jones's at the time, you remember, one Godfrey Pitman. Helstonleigh said, you know,

Miss Rye, that if anybody did it, it was him. That Godfrey Pitman is an uncommonly sharp card to have kept himself out of the way so long! Don't you think so?"

"I don't think anything about it," she answered. "What is it to me?"

"Well, Miss Rye, I've the pleasure of telling you that Godfrey Pitman's found!"

The little presence of mind left in Alletha Rye seemed to quit her at the words. Perhaps she was no longer so capable of maintaining it as she once had been: the very best of our powers wear out when the soul's burthen is continued long and long.

"Found!" she gasped, her hands falling on her work, her wild eyes turned to Mr. Butterby.

"Leastways, so near found, that it mayn't be a age afore he's took," added the detective, with professional craft. "Our friends in the blue coats have got the clue to him. I'd not lay you the worth of that silver thimble of yours, Miss Rye, that he's not standing in a certain dock next March assizes."

"In what dock? What for?" came from her trembling lips.

"Helstonleigh dock. For what he did to Mr. Ollivera. Come, come, I did not want to frighten you like this, my good young woman.

And why should it ? It is not certain Pitman will be brought to trial, though he were guilty. Years have gone by since, and the Greatorexes and Parson Ollivera may hush it up. They are humane men ; Mr. Bede especially."

" *You* don't believe Godfrey Pitman was guilty ?" she exclaimed, and her eyes began to take a hard look, her voice a defiant tone.

" Oh,   don't   I ! "   returned   Butterby. " What's more to the purpose, Miss Rye, the London officers and their principals, who have got it in hand, believe it."

"And what if I tell you that Godfrey Pitman never was guilty ; that he never raised his hand against Mr. Ollivera ?" she broke forth in passionate accents, rising to confront him. " What if I tell you that it was *I* ?"

Standing there before him, her eyes ablaze with light, her cheeks crimson, her voice ringing with power, it was nearly impossible to disbelieve her. For once, the experienced, cool man was taken aback.

" *You*, Miss Rye !"

" Yes, I.   I, Alletha Rye.   What, I say, if I tell you it was I did that terrible deed ? *Not* Godfrey Pitman. Now then ! you must make the most of it, and do your best and worst."

The avowal, together with the various ideas that came crowding as its accompaniment, struck Mr. Butterby dumb. He sat there gazing at her, his speech utterly failing him.

" Is this true ?" he whispered, when he had found his tongue.

" Should I avow such a thing if it were not? Oh, Mr. Butterby! hush the matter up if it be in your power," she implored, clasping her hands in an attitude of beseeching supplication, and her breath came in great gasps, so that the words were jerked out, rather than spoken. " In pity to me, hush it ; it has lain at rest all these years. Let Godfrey Pitman be ! for my sake, let him be ! I pray you, in Heaven's name !"

She sat down in her chair, tottering back to it, and burst into a flood of hysterical tears. Mr. Butterby waited in silence till they were over, and then buttoned his coat to go out. Putting out her timid hand, she caught his arm and held it with a nervous grasp.

" You will promise me, Mr. Butterby ?"

" I can't promise anything on the spur of the moment," said he in a grave, but not unkind tone. " You must let me turn things over in my mind. For one thing, neither the hushing of the matter up, nor the pursuing of it, may lie with me. I told you others had got it in hand, Miss Rye, and I told you truth. Now there's no need for you to come to the door; I can let myself out."

And Mr. Butterby let himself out accordingly, making no noise over the exit.

"I'm *blest* if I can see daylight," he exclaimed with energy, as he went down the street at a brisk pace. "Did she do it herself?—or is she trying to screen Master George Winter? It's one of the two; and I'm inclined to think it is the last. Anyway, she's a brave and a bold woman. Whether she did it, or whether she didn't, it's no light matter to accuse herself of mur——"

Mr. Butterby came to a full stop: both in words and steps. It was but for a second of time; and he laughed a little silent laugh at his own obtuseness as he passed on.

"I forgot her avowal at the grave. If she had done it herself, she'd never have gone in for that public display, lest it should turn attention on her. Yes, yes; she is screening Winter. Perhaps the man, hiding in that top floor, with nothing to do but torment his wits, got jealous of the counsellor below, fancying she favoured him, and so——"

The break in Mr. Butterby's sentence this time was occasioned by his shooting into an entry. Approaching towards him came Mrs. Jones, attended by her servant with a huge market-basket: and as he had neither time nor wish for an encounter with that lady at the present moment, he let her go by.

CHAPTER XXXIV.

THAT same evening, just as suddenly as Detective Butterby had shot into the entry, did he seem to shoot into the private room of Mr. Bede Greatorex. The clerks had just left the office for the evening; Bede, putting things straight on his desk, was thinking of going up stairs to dinner. To be thus silently invaded was not pleasing : but Bede could only resign himself to his fate.

In a spirit of reproach Mr. Butterby entered on the business of the interview, stating certain facts. Bede took alarm. Better, as he thought, that the earth should be arrested in its orbit, than that the part Godfrey Pitman played in connection with his cousin's death at Helstonleigh should be brought to light.

"It is the very charge, above all others, that I gave you, Mr. Butterby—the keeping secret what you had learnt about the identity of Godfrey Pitman," broke forth Bede.

" And it is because I obeyed you and did keep it, that head-quarters have it put into others' hands and are hauling me over the coals," spoke Mr. Butterby in an injured tone.

" Have you told them that it was by my desire you remained passive ?"

" I've told them nothing," was the answer. " I let 'em think that I was looking after Godfrey Pitman still myself, everywhere that I could look, high and low."

" Then they don't know yet that he and my clerk Brown are the same ?" said Bede, very eagerly.

" Not a bit on't. There's not a living soul of the lot has been sharp enough to turn that page yet, Mr. Bede Greatorex."

" And it must be our business to keep it closed," whispered Bede. " I will give you any reward if you can manage to do it."

" Look here, sir," spoke Butterby. " I'm willing to oblige you as far as I can in reason ; I've showed you that I am ; but to fill you up with hopes that that secret will be a secret long, would be nothing but wilful deceit : and deceit's a thing that don't answer in the long run. When I want to throw people off a scent, or worm things out of 'em for the law's purposes, I send their notions off on all sorts of air journeys, and think it no wrong : but to let you suppose I can keep from the world what I can't keep, and take your thanks and rewards for doing it, is just the opposite case. As sure as us two be a talking here, this matter won't stand at its present page; there'll be more leafs turned in it afore many days is gone over."

Leaning forward, his face and eyes wearing their gravest look, his elbow on the table that was between them, his finger and thumb pointed to give force to his argument, there was that altogether in the speaker's aspect, in his words, that carried a shiver of conviction to the mind of Bede Greatorex. His heart grew faint, his face was white with a sickly moisture.

" You may think to stop it and I may think to stop it, Mr. Bede Greatorex : but, take my word, it won't be stopped. There's no longer a chance of it."

" If you—could get—Brown out of the way ?" spoke Bede, scarcely knowing what it was he said, and speaking in a whisper. Mr. Butterby received the suggestion with severity.

" It's not to me, sir, that you should venture to say such a thing. I've been willing to help your views when it didn't lie against my position and duty to do it; but I don't think you've seen anything in me to suppose

I would go beyond that.   As good step into
Scotland Yard and ask *them* to help a criminal
to escape, as ask me.   We'll let that drop,
sir ; and I'll go on to a question I should like
to put.   What do you want Godfrey Pitman
out of the way for ?"

Bede did not answer.   His hand was pressed
upon his brow, his eyes wore their saddest
and most dreamy look.

" If Pitman had any share in the business
at Helstonleigh, you ought to be the one to
give him into custody, sir."

" For the love of Heaven, don't pursue
Pitman !" spoke Bede earnestly.   " I have
told you before, Mr. Butterby, that it was not
he.   So far as I believe, he never lifted his
hand against John Ollivera ; he did not hurt
a hair of his head.   Accuse any one in the
world that you please, but don't accuse him."

" What if I accuse a woman ?" spoke Mr.
Butterby, when he had gazed at Bede to his
satisfaction.

Their eyes met.   Bede's face, or the detective fancied it, was growing whiter.

" Who ?—What woman ?" asked Bede,
scarcely above his breath.

" Alletha Rye."

With a sudden movement, looking like one
of relief, Bede Greatorex dropped his hand

and leaned back in his chair. It was as if
some kind of rest had come to him.

"Why should you bring in Alletha Rye's
name? Do you suspect her?"

"I'm not clear that I do; I'm not clear
that I don't. Any how, I think she stands a
chance of getting accused of it, Mr. Bede
Greatorex."

"Better accuse her than Pitman," said Bede,
who seemed to be again speaking out of his
uncomfortable dream.

Mr. Butterby, inwardly wondering at various matters, and not just yet able to make
them meet in his official mind, rose to con-
clude the interview. A loud bell was ringing up stairs; most probably the announce-
ment of dinner.

"Just a parting word, sir. What I chiefly
stepped in to say, was this. So long as
the case rested in my hands, and Mr. Godfrey Pitman was supposed to have finally disappeared from the world, I was willing to
oblige you, and let it, and him, and the world
be. But from the moment that the affair
shall be stirred publicly, in short, that action
is forced upon me by others, I shall take it
up again. Counsellor Ollivera's case belongs
of right to me, and must be mine to the end."

With a civil good-night, Mr. Butterby de-

parted, leaving Bede Greatorex to his thoughts
and reveries.   More unhappy ones have rarely
been entertained in this world.   Men cannot
strive against fate for ever, and the battle
had well nigh worn him out.   It almost seemed
that he could struggle no longer, that he had
no power of resistance left within him.   Mind
and body were alike weary ; the spirit fainted,
the heart was sick.   Life had long been a
burden to Bede Greatorex, but never did its
weight lie heavier than to-night, in its refined
and exquisite pain.·

He had to bear it alone, you see.   To lock
the miserable secret, whatever might be its
precise nature, and whoever might have been
guilty, within his own bosom.   Could he but
have spoken of it to another, its anguish had
been less keen ; for, when once a great trouble
can be imparted—be it of grief, or apprehension, or remorse ; be it connected with ourselves, or (worse) one very near and dear to
us—it is lightened of half its sting.

But that relief was denied to Bede Greatorex.

It had been the dinner-bell.   Bede did not
answer to it ; but that was not altogether
unusual.

They sat around the brilliantly-lighted,
well-appointed banquet.   Where Mrs. Bede

Greatorex procured her fresh hot-house flowers from daily, and at what cost, she alone knew. They were always beautiful, charming to the eye, odoriferously pleasant to the senses. At the head of the table to-night was she, wearing amber silk, her shoulders very bare, her back partially shaded by the horse's tail that drooped from her remarkable chignon. It was not a dinner-party; but Mrs. Bede was going out later, and had dressed beforehand.

The place at her left-hand was vacant— Bede's—who never took the foot of the table when his father was present. Mr. Greatorex supposed his son was detained in the office, and sent a servant to see. Judge Kene sat on the right of Mrs. Bede; he had called in, and stayed to dinner without ceremony. Clare Joliffe and Miss Channing sat on either side Mr. Greatorex. Frank was dining out. Clare was returning to France for Christmas, after her many months' stay in the country. Her chignon was more fashionable than a quartern loaf, and certainly larger, but lacking that great achievement, the tail. Annabel's quiet head presented a contrast to those two of the mode.

Bede came up. Shaking hands with Sir Thomas Kene, he passed round to his chair; his manner was restless, his thin cheeks were hectic. The judge had not seen him for some little time. Gazing at him across the table, he wondered what malady he could be suffering from, and how much more like a shadow he would be able to become—and live. Mr. Greatorex, anxiously awake to every minute glance or motion bearing on his son's health, spoke.

"Are you thinking Bede looks worse, Sir Thomas?"

"He does not look better," was the reply. "You should see a doctor and take some tonics, Bede."

"I am all right, Judge, thank you," was Bede's answer, as he turned a whole lot of croûtons into his purée de pois—and would afterwards send it away nearly untasted.

Dinner was just over when a servant whispered to Mr. Greatorex that he was wanted. Going down at once to his room he found Henry William Ollivera.

"Why did you not come up, William? Kene is there."

"I am in no fit mood for company, uncle," was the clergyman's reply. "The trouble has come at last."

In all the phases of agitation displayed by Henry Ollivera, and when speaking of the affair he generally displayed more or less, Mr.

Greatorex never saw him so much moved as now. Leaning forward on his chair, his eyes bright, his cheeks burning as with the red of an autumn leaf, his hands feverish, his voice sunk to a whisper, he entered on the tale he had to tell.

"Do you remember my saying to you one day in the dining-room above, that I thought it was a woman? Do you remember it, uncle?"

"Quite well."

"In the weeks that have gone by since, the suspicion has only gained ground in my mind. Without cause: I am bound to say it, without further cause. Nay, almost in the teeth of what might have served to diminish suspicion. For, if Godfrey Pitman be really somewhere in existence, and hiding himself, the natural supposition would be, as Jelf thinks, that *he* was the one."

Mr. Greatorex nodded assent. "And yet you suspect the woman! Can you not say who she is, Henry?"

"Yes, I can say now. I have come here to say it—Alletha Rye!"

Mr. Greatorex evinced no surprise. He had fancied it might be upon her that his nephew's doubts had been running. And he deemed it a crotchet indeed.

"I think you must be entirely mistaken," he said with emphasis. "What little I know of the young woman, tends to give me a very high opinion of her. She appears to be almost the last person in the world capable of such a crime as that, or of any crime."

"She might have done it in a moment's passion; she might have been playing with the pistol and fired it accidentally, and then was afraid to avow it : but she *did* it, uncle."

"Go on."

"I have been distracted with doubt. Distracted," emphatically repeated Mr. Ollivera. "For of course I knew that my suspicions of her, strong though they have been growing, did not prove her guilty. But to-night I have heard her avow it with her own lips."

"Avow what ?"

"That she murdered John !"

"What !—has she confessed to you ?" exclaimed Mr. Greatorex.

"No. I heard it accidentally. Perhaps I ought to say surreptitiously. And, hearing it in that manner, the question arises in my mind whether or not I should make use of the knowledge so gained. I cannot bear anything like dishonourable or under-hand dealing; no, not even in this cause, uncle."

Mr. Greatorex made no reply. He was

taken up with noting the strangely eager gaze fixed on him. Something in it, he knew not what, recalled to his memory a dead face, lying alone on the border of a distant church-yard.

"It is some few weeks ago now that Mrs. Jones gave me a latch-key," resumed Mr. Ollivera. "In fact, I asked her for it. Coming in so often, and sometimes detained out late at night with the sick, I felt that it would be a convenience to me, and save trouble to the maid. This evening, upon letting myself in with it about tea-time, I found the passage in darkness; the girl, I supposed, had delayed to light the lamp. My movements are not noisy at any time, as you know, and I went groping on in silence, feeling my way: not from any wish to be stealthy—such a thought never entered my head—but because Mr. Roland Yorke is given to leave all kinds of articles about and I was afraid of stumbling over something. I was making for the table at the end of the passage, on which matches are generally kept, sometimes a chamber-candle. Feeling for these, I heard a voice in Mrs. Jones's parlour that I have not heard many times in my life, but nevertheless I knew it instantly—Butterby's, the detective."

"Butterby's!" exclaimed Mr. Greatorex. "I did not know he was in London."

"Uncle! It was Alletha Rye's voice that answered him. Her voice, and no other's, disguised with agitation though it was. I heard her say that it was herself who killed my brother; that Godfrey Pitman had never raised a hand against him."

"You—really heard her say this, William?" breathed Mr. Greatorex.

"It is true as that I am a living man. It seemed to me that the officer must have been accusing Godfrey Pitman of the crime. I heard the man's surprised answer 'You, Miss Rye!' I heard her again reiterate her self-accusing avowal. 'Yes, I,' she said, 'I, Alletha Rye, *not* Godfrey Pitman.' I heard her go on to tell Butterby that he might do his best and his worst."

Mr. Greatorex sat like one bereft of motion. "This confounds me, William," he presently said.

"It confounded me," replied Mr. Ollivera. "Nearly took my senses from me, for I'm sure I had no rational reason left. The first thought that came to me was, that they had better not see me there, or discover they had been overheard, until I had decided what my course should be. So I stepped silently up to my room, and the detective went away; and, close upon that, Mrs. Jones and the maid came in together. Mrs. Jones called her sister to account for not having lighted the hall-lamp, little thinking how the darkness had served me."

"But for your telling me this yourself, William, I had not believed it."

"It is true as Heaven's gospel," spoke the clergyman in his painful earnestness. "I sat a short while in my room, unable to decide what I ought to do, and then I came down here to tell you of it, uncle. It is very awful."

"Awful that it should have been Alletha Rye, you mean?"

"Yes. I have been praying, seeking, working for this discovery ever since John died; and, now that it has come in this most sudden manner, it brings nothing but perplexity with it. Oh, poor helpless mortals that we are!" added the clergyman, clasping his hands. "We set our hearts upon some longed-for end, spend our days toiling for it, our nights supplicating for it; and when God answers us according to our short-sighted wish, the result is but as the apples of Sodom, filling our mouths with ashes. Anybody but Alletha Rye; almost anybody; and I had not hesitated a moment. But I have lived under the same roof with her, in pleasant, friendly intercourse ; I have preached to her on Sundays ; I have given her Christ's Holy Sacrament with my own hands : in a serious illness that she had, I used to go and pray by her bedside. Oh, Uncle Greatorex, I cannot see where my duty lies ; I am torn with conflicting doubt !"

To the last words Mr. Ollivera had a listener that he had not bargained for—Judge Kene. About to take his departure, the Judge had come in without ceremony to say Good-night to Mr. Greatorex.

"Why, what is amiss ?" he cried, noting the signs of agitation as well as the words.

And they told him ; told him all ; there was no reason why it should be kept from him ; and Mr. Ollivera begged for his counsel and advice. The Judge gave it, and most emphatically ; deciding *as* a judge more than as a humane man—and Thomas Kene was that.

"You cannot hesitate, Ollivera. This poor unhappy woman, Alletha Rye, must be brought to answer for her crime. Think of *him*, your brother, and my once dear friend, lying unavenged in his shameful grave ! Humanity is a great and a good virtue, but John's memory must out-weigh it."

"Yes, yes; I am thinking of him always," murmured the clergyman, his face lighting.

"The initiative was taken by Mr. Greatorex. On the departure of the Judge and the clergyman, who went out together, Mr. Greatorex dropped a line to Scotland Yard. Butterby happened to be there, and answered it in person. Shortly and concisely Mr. Greatorex gave his orders.

"And I have no resource but to act upon them," coolly observed the imperturbable Butterby. "But I don't think the party was Alletha Rye."

"You don't!" exclaimed Mr. Greatorex.

"No, sir, I don't. Leastways, to my mind, there's grave reasons against it. The whole affair, from beginning to end, seems encompassed with nothing but doubts; and that's the blessed truth."

"I would like to ask you if Alletha Rye has or has not made a confession to you this evening, Mr. Butterby—to the effect that she was the one who killed Mr. Ollivera?"

"If nobody was in the house but her—as she said—she's been talking," thought the detective. "Confound these women for simpletons! They'd prate their necks away."

But Mr. Greatorex was looking at him, waiting for the answer.

"I was with Alletha Rye this evening; I went there for my own purposes, to see what I could get out of her; little suspecting she'd say what she did. But I don't believe her any the more for having said it. The fact is, Mr. Greatorex, that in this case there's wheels within wheels, a'most more than in any I've ever had to do with. I can't yet disclose what they are, even to you; but I'm trying to work them round and make one spoke fit into another."

"Do you *know* that Alletha Rye was not guilty of it?"

"No, sir, I do not."

"Very good. Lose no time. Get a warrant to apprehend Alletha Rye, and execute it. If you telegraph to Helstonleigh at once, the warrant may be up, and she in custody before midday to-morrow."

No more dallying with the law or with fate now. That was over. Mr. Butterby went straight to the telegraph office, and sent a message flying to Helstonleigh.

And Bede Greatorex went out to take part in an evening's gaiety with his wife, and came home to his rest, and rose the next morning to go about his occupation, unconscious of what the day was destined to bring forth.

CHAPTER XXXV.

A COLD brisk air, with suspicion of a frost. It was a day or two previous to the one told of in the last two chapters, when Mr. Butterby was paying visits. Being convenient to record that renowned officer's doings first, we yielded him the precedence, and in consequence have to go back a little.

The brightness of the afternoon was passing. In his writing-room, leaning back in a large easy-chair before the fire, sat Hamish Channing. Some papers lay on the table, work of various kinds; but, looking at Hamish, it almost seemed as though he had done with work for ever. A face less beautiful than Hamish Channing's would have appeared painfully thin : his, spite of its wasted aspect, had yet a wondrous charm. The remark was once made that Hamish Channing's was a face that would be beautiful always; beautiful to the end; beautiful in dying. See it now. The perfect contour of the features is shown the plainer in their attenuation ; the skin seems transparent, the cheeks are delicately flushed, the eyes are very blue and bright. If the countenance had looked etherealized earlier in the history, and any cavilled at the word, they would scarcely have cavilled at it now. But in the strangely spiritual expression, speaking, one knew not how, of Heaven, there was an ever-present sadness, as if trouble had been hard at work with him ; as if all that was of the earth, earthy, had been *crucified* away.

Nobody seemed certain of it yet—that he was dying, He bore up bravely ; working still a little at home ; but not going to the office ; that was beyond him. The doctors had not said there was no hope : his wife, though she might inwardly feel how it was, would not speak it. He sat at the head of his table yet ; he was careful of his appearance as of yore. His smile was genial still ; his loving words were cheerful, sometimes gay ; his sweet kindliness to all around was more marked. Oh, it was not in the face only that the look of Heaven appeared : if ever a spark of the Divine spirit of love and light had been vouchsafed to man's soul, it surely had been to that of Hamish Channing.

He wore a coat of black velvet, a vest of

the same, across which his gold chain passed, with its drooping seal. The ring, formerly Mr. Channing's, no longer made believe to fit the little finger; it was worn on the second. His hair, carefully brushed as ever, looked like threads of dark gold in the sunlight. Certainly it could not be said that Hamish gave in to his illness. Whatever his complaint might be, the medical men did not call it by any name; there was a little cough, a strange want of tone and strength, a quick, continual, almost perceptible wasting. Whether Hamish had cherished visions of recovery for himself could not be known; most earnestly he had hoped for it. If only for the sake of his wife and child, he desired to live : and existence itself, even in the midst of a great and crushing disappointment, is hard to resign. But the truth, long dawning on his mind, had shown itself to him fully at last, as it does in similar cases to most of us; whether Hamish's weakness had taken a stride, and brought conviction of its formidable nature, or whether it might be that he was temporarily feeling worse, a sadness, as of death itself, lay upon him this afternoon.

It had been a short life—as men count lives; he had not yet numbered two and thirty years. But for the awful disappointment that was drying its fibres away, he might say that it had been a supremely happy one. Perhaps no man, with the sweet and sunny temperament of Hamish Channing, possessing the same Christian principles, could be otherwise than happy. He did not remember ever to have done ill wilfully to mortal man, in thought, word, or deed. It had been done to him : but he forgave it. Nevertheless, a sense of injustice, a bitter pang of disappointment, of hopeless failure as to this world, lay on his heart, when he recalled what the past few months had brought him. Leaning there on his chair, his sad eyes tracing figures in the fire, he was recalling things one by one. His never-ceasing, ever-hopeful work, and the bright dreams of future fame that had made its sunshine. He remembered, as though it were to-day, the evening that first review met his eye—when he had been entertaining his brother-in-law, the Reverend William Yorke, and others—and the shock it gave him. Think of it when he would even now, it brought him a sensation of sick faintness. Older men have become paralyzed from a similar shock. That first review had been so closely followed by others, equally unjust, equally cruel, that they all seemed as one blow. After that there appeared to be a sort of pause in his life, when time and events stood still, when he moved as one in a dream of misery, when all things around him were as dead, and he along with them. The brain (as it seemed) never stopped beating, or the bosom's pain working; or the sense of humiliation to quit him. And then, as the days went on, bodily weakness supervened; and—there he was, dying. Dying! going surely to his God and Saviour; he felt that; but leaving his dear ones, wife and child, to the frowns of a hard world; alone, without suitable provision. And the book—the good, scholarly, attractive book, upon which he had bestowed the best of his bright genius, that he had written as to Heaven—was lying unread. Wasted!

"Papa, shall I put on her blue frock or her green? She is going out for a walk."

The interruption came from Miss Nelly, who sat on the hearth-rug, dressing her doll. There was no reply, and Nelly looked up: she wore a blue frock herself; its sleeves and the white pinafore tied together with blue ribbon. Her pretty little feet in their shoes and socks were stretched out, and her curls fell in a golden shower.

"Shall baby wear her blue frock or her green, papa? Papa, then! Which is prettiest?"

Hamish, aroused, looked down on the child with a smile. "The blue, I think ; and then baby-doll will be like Nelly."

But Mrs. Channing, sewing at the window, turned her head. Something in her husband's face or in his weary tone struck her.

"Do you feel worse, Hamish ?"

"No, love. Not particularly."

Sadder yet, the voice ; a kind of hopeless, weary sadness, depressing to hear. Ellen quitted her seat, and came to him.

"What is it ?" she whispered.

"Not much, dear. The future has cleared itself, that's all."

"The future ?"

"I cannot struggle any longer, Ellen. I have preached faith and patience to others, but they seem to have deserted me. I—I almost think the very strife itself is helping on the end."

Sharp though the pang was, that pierced her breast, she would not show it. Miss Nelly chattered below, asking questions of her doll, and making believe to answer.

"The —— end, Hamish !"

He took her hand and looked straight in her face as she stood by him. "Have you not seen it, Ellen ?"

With a heart and bosom that alike qui-

vered,—with a standing still of all her pulses,
—with a catching-up of breath, as a sob, Mrs.
Channing was conscious of a stab of pain.
Oh yes—yes—she had seen it; and the per-
suading herself that she had not, had been
but a sickly, miserable pretence at cheating.

"But for leaving you and the little one,
Ellen, there would be no strife," he whispered,
letting his forehead rest for a moment on her
arm. "It is a long while now that my
dreams—I had almost said my visions—have
been of that world to which we are all jour-
neying, which every one of us must enter
sooner or later. There will be no pain, or
trouble, or weariness *there*. Only the other
night, as I lay between sleep and wake, I
seemed to have passed its portals into a soft,
bright, soothing light, a haven of joyous peace
and rest."

"And if dolly's good, and does not spoil
her new blue frock, she shall go out for a
walk," was heard from the hearth-rug. Hamish put his elbow on the arm of the chair,
and covered his face with his slender fingers.

"But when I think of my wife and child—
and I am always thinking of them, Ellen,—
when I realise the bitter truth that I must
leave them, why then at times it seems as if
my heart must break with its intense pain.

Ellen, my darling, I would not, even yet, have spoken, but that I know you must have been waiting for it."

"I could have borne any trouble better than this," she answered, pressing her hands together.

"It will he softened to you, I am sure, Ellen. I am ever praying that it may."

"But ——"

Visitors in the drawing-room : Mrs. Bede Greatorex and Miss Joliffe. A servant came to announce them. She had said that her mistress was at home, and Ellen had to go up. Hamish, with his remaining strength, lifted Miss Nelly on his knee, doll and all.

"Hush, papa, please ! Baby is fatigued with making her toilette. She wants to go to sleep."

"What would Nelly say if papa told her he also wanted to go to sleep ?"

Miss Nelly lay back in papa's arms while she considered the question, the doll hushed in hers. Ah me, it is ever thus ! We clasp and love our children : they love others, who are more to them than we are.

"Why ? Are you tired, papa ?"

"A little weary, dear."

"Then go to sleep. Doll shall be quiet."

"The sleep's not coming just yet, Nelly.

And—when it does come—papa may not awake from it."

"Not ever, ever, ever?" asked Nelly, opening her blue eyes in wonder, but not taking in at all the true sense of the question.

"Not ever—here."

"The princess went into a sleep in my tale-book, and lay on the bed with roses in her hair, and never awoke, never, never, till the good old fairy came and touched her," said Miss Nelly.

There ensued a pause. Hamish Channing's lip quivered a little ; but no one, save himself, could have guessed how every fibre of his heart was aching.

"Nelly," he resumed, his voice and manner alike gravely earnest, his eyes reading hers, "I want to give you a charge. Should papa have to go on a long journey, you would be all that mamma has left. Take you care, my child, to be ever dutiful to her ; to be obedient to her slightest wish, and to love her with a double love."

"A long, long, long journey?" demanded Miss Nelly.

"Very long."

"And when would you come back again to this house?"

"Not ever."

" Where would it be to, papa ?"

" Heaven," he softly whispered.

Nelly rose up in his arms, the blue eyes more wondering than before.

" But that would be to die !"

" And if it were ?"

Down fell the doll unheeded. The child's fears were aroused. She threw her little arms about his neck.

" Oh papa, papa, don't die ! Don't die !"

" But if I must, Ellen ?"

Only once in her whole life could she remember that he had called her by her true name, and that was when her grandpapa died. She began to tremble.

" Who would take care of me, papa ?"

" God."

She hid her face upon his velvet waistcoat, strangely still.

" He would guide, and guard, and love you ever, Ellen. Loving Him, you would be His dear child always, and He would bring you in time to me. Look up, my dear one."

" *Must* you go the journey ?"

" I fear so."

" Oh, papa !—and don't you care—don't you care for mamma and me, that you must leave us ?"

" Care !"

He could say no more ; the word seemed to put the finishing stroke to his breaking heart. Sobs broke from his lips ; tears, such as man rarely sheds, streamed down on the little nestling head. A cry of anguish, patient and imploring, that the parting might be soothed to them all, went up aloft to his Father in Heaven.

After dusk came on, when the visitors were got rid of,—for Clare Joliffe had stayed an unconscionable time, talking over old interests at Helstonleigh—Mrs. Channing found her husband asleep in his chair. Closing the door softly on him, she sat down by the dining-room fire, and the long pent-up tears burst forth. Hamish Channing's wife was a brave woman : but there are griefs that go well-nigh, when they fall, to shatter the bravest of us. Miss Nelly, captured ever so long ago by nurse, was at tea in the nursery.

Roland Yorke surprised Mrs. Channing in her sorrow. Roland never came into the house with a clatter now (at least when he thought of its master's sick state), but with as softly decorous a step as his boots could be controlled to. Down he sat in silence, on the opposite side of the hearth, and saw the reflection of Mrs. Channing's tears in the firelight.

"Is he worse?" asked Roland, when he had stared a little.

"No," she answered, scarcely making a pretence to conceal her grief. "I fear there will not be very much 'worse' in it at all, Roland: a little more weakness perhaps, and that will be all. I am afraid the end is very near. I fancy he thinks so."

Roland grew hot and cold; a dart took him under his waistcoat.

"Let's understand, Mrs. Channing. Don't play with a fellow. Do you mean that Hamish is—going—to die?"

"Yes, I am sure there is no more hope."

"My goodness!"—and Roland rubbed his hot and woe-stricken face. "Why he was better yesterday. He was laughing and talking like anything."

"Not really better. It is as I say, Roland."

"If ever I saw such a miserable world as this!" exclaimed Roland: who, though indulging at times some private despondency upon the case, had perhaps not realized its utter hopelessness until now, when the words put it unmistakably before him. "I never thought—at least, much—but what he'd get well again: the fine, good, handsome man.

I'd like to know why he couldn't, and what has killed him."

"The reviews have done it," said Ellen, in a low tone.

Roland groaned. A suspicion, that they must have had something to do with the decay, had been upon himself. Hamish had never been quite the same after they appeared : his spirit had seemed to fade away in a subdued sadness, and subsequently his health followed it.

"The cruel reviews broke his heart," resumed Mrs. Channing. "I am certain of it, Roland. A less sensitive man would not have felt it vitally ; a man, physically stronger, could not have suffered in health. But he is sensitive amidst the most sensitive ; and he never, with all his bright face and fine form, was physically strong. And so—he could not bear the blow, and it has killed him."

Roland sat pulling at his whiskers in desperate gloom. Mrs. Channing shaded her eyes with her hand.

"If I could but pitch into the reviewers !" he cried. "Were I rich, I'd offer a thousand pounds' reward to anybody who would bring me their names. Hang the lot ! And if you were not by, Mrs. Channing, it's a worse word than that I'd say."

She shook her head. "Pitching into the reviewers, Roland, would not give him back his life. The publisher thinks that one man wrote them all : or got them written. Some one who must have had a grudge against Hamish. It does seem like it."

Roland's picture might have been taken as an emblem of Despair. Suddenly the face brightened a little, the sanguine temperament resumed its sway.

"Don't you lose heart, Mrs. Channing. I'll tell you something that happened to me at Port Natal. Uncommon hard-up, I was, and lying in a place with a strong fever upon me. I thought I was dying ; I did indeed. I was dreaming of Helstonleigh and all the old people there ; I seemed to see Arthur and Hamish, and Hamish smiled at me in his bright way, and said 'Cheer up, it will be all right, old friend.' Upon that, somebody was standing by the bed—which was nothing but a sack of sand that you rolled off unpleasantly—laying hold of my pulse and looking down at me. I mean really, you know. A chap in the room said it was a doctor ; perhaps it was ; but he got me nothing but some herb-tea to drink. 'Take courage,' says he to me, ' it's half the battle !' I got well in time, and so may Hamish. *You* take courage, Mrs. Channing."

She smiled a little. "My taking courage would not help my husband, Roland."

"Well—no; perhaps it mightn't," acknowledged Roland, resuming his gloom. "Where is he?"

She pointed to the other room. "Asleep before the fire."

Roland softly opened the door and looked in. The fire-light played on Hamish Channing's wasted features; and his dreams seemed to be of a pleasant nature, for a smile sat on the delicate lips: lips that had always shown so plainly the man's remarkable refinement. Nevertheless, sleeping and dreaming peacefully, there was something in the face that spoke of coming death. And Roland could have burst into sobs as he stood there.

Going back again, and closing the door quietly, Roland found the company augmented in the person of his brother Gerald. For some time past Gerald Yorke had heard from one and another of Hamish Channing's increased illness, which made no impression upon him, except a slightly favourable one; for, if Hamish were incapacitated from writing, it would be a rival removed from Gerald's path. This afternoon he was told that

Hamish was thought to be past recovery; in fact, dying. That did arouse him a little; the faint spark of conscience Gerald Yorke possessed took a twinge, and he thought as he was near the house he'd give a call in.

"You are quite a stranger," Mrs. Channing was saying, meeting Gerald with a cordial hand and a grasp of welcome. "What has kept you away?"

"Aw—been busy of late; and—aw—worried," answered Gerald, according a distant nod to Roland. "What's this I hear about Hamish?—That he is dying!"

"Well, I don't think you need blurt out that strong word to Mrs. Channing, Gerald," interposed hot Roland. "Dying, indeed! Do you call it manners? I don't."

"I beg Mrs. Channing's pardon," Gerald was beginning, half cynically; but Ellen's voice rose to interrupt.

"It makes no difference, Roland," she kindly said. "It is the truth, you know; and I am not blind to it."

"What's the matter with him?" asked Gerald.

The matter with him? Ellen Channing told the brief story in a few words. The cruel reviews had broken his heart. Gerald listened, and felt himself turn into a white heat inside and out.

"The reviews!" he exclaimed. "I don't understand you, Mrs. Channing."

"Of course you read them, Gerald, and must know their bitter, shameful injustice," she explained. "They were such that might have struck a blow even to a strong man: they struck a fatal one to Hamish. He had staked his whole heart and hope upon the book; he devoted to it the great and good abilities with which God had gifted him; he made it worthy of all praise; and false men rose up and blasted it. A strong word you may deem that, Gerald, for me to use; but it is a true one. They rose up, and—in envy, as I believe—set themselves to write and work out a deliberate lie: they got it sent forth to the world in effectual channels, and *killed* the book. Perhaps they did not intend also to kill the writer."

Gerald's white face looked whiter than usual. His eyes, in their hard stare, were very ugly.

"Still I can't understand," he said. "The critiques were, of course, rather severe: but how can critiques kill a man?"

"And if you, being a reviewer yourself, Gerald, could only get to find out who the false-hearted hound was,—for it's thought to

have been one fellow who penned the lot—
you'd oblige me," put in Roland. "I'd *repay*
him, as I've seen it done at Port Natal. His
howling would be something fine."

"You do not yet entirely understand, I see,
Gerald," sadly answered Ellen, paying no attention to Roland's interruption, while Gerald
turned his shoulder upon him. "In one sense
the reviews did not kill. They did not, for
instance, strike Hamish dead at once, or break
his heart with a stroke. In fact, you may
think the expression, a broken heart, but a
figure of speech ; and in a degree of course it
is so. But there are some natures, and his is
one, which are so sensitively organized that a
cruel blow shatters them. Had Hamish been
stronger he might have borne it, have got
over it in time ; but he had been working beyond his strength ; and I think also his
strangely eager hope in regard to the book
must have helped to wear out his frame. It
was his first work, you know. When the
blow came he had not strength to rally from
it ; mind and body were alike stricken down,
and so the weakness set in and laid hold of
him."

"What are these natures good for ?" fiercely
demanded Gerald, in a tone as if he were resenting some personal injury.

"Only for Heaven, as it seems to me," she gently answered.

Gerald rubbed his face; he could not get any colour into it, and there ensued a pause. Presently Ellen spoke again.

"I remember, when I was quite a girl, reading of a somewhat similar case in one of Bulwer Lytton's novels. A young artist painted a great picture—great to him—and insisted on being concealed in the room while a master came to judge of it. The judgment was adverse; not, perhaps, particularly harsh and cruel in itself, only sounding so to the painter; and it killed him. Not at the moment, Gerald; I don't mean that; he lived to become ill, and he went to Italy for his health, his heart gradually breaking. He never spoke of what the blow had been to him, or that it had crushed out his hope and life, but died hiding it. Hamish has never spoken."

"What I want to know is, where's the use of people being like this?" pursued Gerald. "What are they made for?"

"Scarcely for earth," she answered. "The too-exquisitely-refined gold is not meant for the world's coinage."

"I'd rather be a bit of brittle china, than made so that I couldn't stand a review," said

Gerald. "It's to be hoped there's not many such people."

"Only one in tens of thousands, Gerald."

"Does it — trouble him?" asked Gerald, hesitatingly.

"The advance of death?—yes, in a degree. Not for the death, Gerald: but the quitting me and Nelly."

"I'm not yet what Hamish and Arthur are, safe to be heard up there when they ask for a thing," again interrupted Roland, jerking his head upwards: "but I do pray that from the day that bad base man hears of Hamish Channing's death, he'll be haunted by his ghost for ever. My goodness! I'd not like to have murder on *my* conscience. It's as bad as the fellow who killed Mr. Ollivera."

Gerald Yorke rose. Ellen asked him to wait and see Hamish, but he answered, in what seemed a desperate hurry, that he had an engagement.

"You might like to take a peep at him, Gerald," spoke Roland. "His face looks as peaceful as if it were sainted."

Gerald's answer was to turn tail and go off. Roland, who had some copying on hand that was being waited for, stayed to shake hands with Mrs. Channing.

"Look here," he whispered to her. "Don't

you let him worry his mind about you and Nelly : in the way of money, you know. I shall be sure to get into something good soon ; Vincent will see to that ; and I'll take care of both of you. Good-bye."

Poor, penniless, good-hearted Roland ! He would have " taken care " of all the world.

With a run he caught up Gerald, who was striding along rapidly. Oblivious of all save the present distress, even of Gerald's past coldness, Roland attempted to take his arm. And got repulsed for his pains.

" My way does not lie the same as yours, I think," was Gerald's haughty remark. Roland would not resent it.

" I say, Ger, is it not enough to make one sad ? It wouldn't have mattered much had it been you or me to be taken : but Hamish Channing ! we can't afford to lose such a one as him."

" Thank you," said Gerald. " Speak for yourself."

" And with Hamish the bread and cheese dies. She has but little money. Perhaps she'll not feel the want of it, though. I'd work my arms off for that darling little Nelly —and for her too, for Hamish's sake."

" I don't believe he is dying at all," said Gerald. " Reviews kill him, indeed ! it's altogether preposterous.   Women talk wretched nonsense in this world."

Without so much as a parting Good-night, Gerald struck across the street and disappeared.   By the time he arrived at his chambers, his mind had fully persuaded itself that there was nothing serious the matter with Hamish Channing : and he felt that he could like to shake Winny (who had been *his* informant) for alarming him.

His servant brought him a letter as he entered, and Gerald tore it open.   It proved to be from Sir Vincent Yorke, inviting Gerald down to Sunny Mead on the morrow for a couple of days' shooting.

" Hurrah !" shouted Gerald.   " Vin's coming round, is he !   I'll go, and get out of him a hundred or so, to bring back with me to town. That's good.   Hurrah !"

CHAPTER XXXVI.

GERALD YORKE AT A SHOOTING PARTY.

It was a pretty place; its name, Sunny Mead, an appropriate one. For the bright sun (not far yet above the horizon) of the clear and cold December day, shone on it cheerily: on the walls of the dwelling-house—on the green grass of the spreading lawn, with its groups of flowering laurestina and encompassing trees, that in summer cast a grateful shade. The house was small, but compact; the prospect from the windows, with its expanse of wood and hill and dale, a charming one. At its best it was a simple, unpretending place, but as pleasant a homestead for moderate desires as could be found in the county of Surrey.

In a snug room, its fire blazing in the grate, its snowy breakfast cloth, laden with china and silver, drawn near the large window that looked upon the lawn, sat the owner, Sir Vincent Yorke, and his cousin Gerald. As soon as breakfast should be over, they were going out shooting; but the baronet was by no means one who liked to disturb his morning's comfort by starting at dawn: shooting, as well as everything else in life, he liked to take easily. Gerald had arrived the previous night: it was the first time Gerald had seen Sunny Mead; and the very unpretending rank it took amidst baronets' dwelling-places, surprised him. Sir Vincent's marriage was fixed for the following month, January; and he gratified Gerald much by saying that he thought of asking him to be groomsman.

"Aw!—very happy—immensely so," responded Gerald with his most fashionable drawl, that so grated on a true and honest ear.

"Sunny Mead has this advantage; one can come to it and be quiet," observed Sir Vincent. "There's not room for more than three or four servants in it. My father used to call it the homestead: that's just what it is, and it doesn't pretend to be aught else. More coffee? Try that partridge pie. Have you seen Roland lately?"

The cynical expression of disparagement that pervaded Gerald's face at the question, made Sir Vincent smile.

"Aw—I say, don't you spoil my breakfast

by bringing up *him*," spoke Gerald. "The best thing he can do is to go out to Port Natal again. A capital pie!"

"This devilled turkey's good, too. You'll try it presently?" spoke the baronet. "How is Hamish Channing?"

Gerald's skin turned of a dark hue. Was Sir Vincent purposely annoying him? Catching up his coffee-cup to take a long draught, he did not answer.

"I never saw so fine a fellow in all my life," resumed Sir Vincent. "Never was so taken with a face at first sight as with his. William Yorke was staying there at the time of my father's funeral, and I went next day to call. That's how I saw Channing. He promised to come and see me; but somebody told me the other day he was ill."

"Aw—yes," drawled Gerald. "Seedy, I believe."

"What's the matter with him?"

"Temper," said Gerald. "Wrote a book, and had some reviews upon it, and it put him out, I hear."

"But it was a first-rate book, Gerald; I read it, and the reviews were all wrong: suppose some contemptible raven of envy scrawled them. The book's working its way upwards as fast as it can now."

" Who says so ?" cried Gerald.

" I do. I had the information from a reliable source. By-the-way, is there anything in that story of Roland's—that he is engaged to Channing's sister ? or is it fancy ?"

" I do wish you'd let the fellow's name be ; he's not so very good to talk of," retorted Gerald, in a rage.

But Roland was not so easily put out of the conversation. As luck had it, when the servant brought Sir Vincent's letters in, there was one from Roland amidst them. Vincent laughed outright as he read it :—

" DEAR VINCENT,

 " I happened to overhear old Greatorex say yesterday that Sir Vincent Yorke wanted a working bailiff for the land at Sunny Mead. I ! wish ! to ! offer ! myself ! for ! the ! situation ! There ! I put it strong that you may not mistake. Of course, I am a relative, which I can't help being ; and a working bailiff is but a kind of upper servant. But I'll be very glad of the place if you'll give it me, and will do my duty in it as far as I can, putting my best shoulder to the wheel ; and I'll never presume upon our being cousins to go into your house uninvited, or put myself in your way ; and my wife would not call on Lady

Yorke if she did not wish it. I'll be the bailiff
—you the master.

" I don't tell you I am a first hand at farming; but, if perseverance and sticking to work
can teach, I shall soon learn it. I picked up
some experience at Port Natal; and had to
drive waggons and other animals. I'm great
in pigs. The droves I had to manage of the
grunting, obstinate wretches, out there, taught
me enough of them. Of course I know all
about hay-making; and I'd used to be one of
the company at old Pierce's harvest homes, on
his farm near Helstonleigh. I don't suppose
you'd want me to thresh the wheat myself;
but I'm strong to do it, and would not mind.
I would be always up before dawn in spring
to see to the young lambs; and I'd soon
acquire the ins and outs of manuring and
draining. Do try me, Vincent! I'll put my
shoulder to the wheel in earnest for you.
There'd be one advantage in taking me—that
I should be honest and true to your interests.
Whereas some bailiffs like to serve themselves
better than their masters.

"As to wages, I'd leave that to you. You'd
not give less than a hundred a year to begin
with ; and at the twelvemonth's end, when I
had made myself qualified, you might make it

two. Perhaps you'd give the two hundred at once. I don't wish to presume because I am a relative; and if the two hundred would be too much at first (for, to tell the truth, I don't know how bailiffs' pay runs), please excuse my having named it. I expect there are lots of pretty cottages to be hired down there; may be there's one on the estate appropriated to the bailiff. I may as well mention that I am a first-rate horseman, and could gallop about like a fire-engine; having nearly lost my life more times than one, learning to ride the wild cattle when up the country at Port Natal.

"I think that's all I have to say. Only try me! If you do, you will find how willing I am. Besides being strong, I am naturally active, with plenty of energy: the land should not go to ruin for the want of being looked after. My object in life now is to get a certainty that will bring me in something tolerably good to begin, and go on to three hundred a year, or more; for I should not like Annabel to take pupils always. I don't know whether a bailiff ever gets as much.

"Bede Greatorex can give you a good character of me for steadiness and industry. And if I have stuck to this work, I should do better by yours; for writing I hate, and knocking about a farm I'd like better than anything.

"You'll let me have an answer as soon as convenient. If you take me I shall have to order leggings and other suitable toggery from Carrick's tailor; and he might be getting on with the things.

"Wishing you a merry Christmas, which will soon be here (don't I recollect one of mine at Port Natal, when I had nothing for dinner and the same for supper), I remain, dear Vincent,

"Yours truly,

"ROLAND YORKE."

"Sir Vincent Yorke."

To watch the curl of Gerald's lips, the angry sarcasm of his face, as he perused this document, which the baronet handed to him with a laugh, was amusing. It might have made a model of scorn for a painter's easel. Dropping the letter from his fingers, as if there were contamination in its very touch, he flicked it across the table.

"You'll send it back to him in a blank envelope, won't you?"

"No; why should I?" returned Sir Vincent, who was good-natured in the main, easy on the whole. " I'll answer him when I've time. Do you know, Gerald, I think you rather disparage Roland."

Gerald opened his astonished eyes. "Disparage him! How *can* he be disparaged?—he is just as low as he can be. An awful blot, and nothing else, on the family escutcheon."

" The family don't seem to be troubled much by him—saving me.   He appears to regard me as a sheet-anchor—who can provide for the world, himself included.   I rather like the young fellow ; he is so genuine."

" Don't call him young," reproved Gerald ; " he'll be twenty-nine next May."

" And in mind and manners he is nineteen !"

" He talks of pigs—see what he has brought *his* to," exclaimed Gerald, somewhat forgetting his fashion.   " The—aw—low kind of work he condescends to do—the mean way he is not ashamed to confess he lives in !   Every bit of family pride has gone out of him, and given place to vulgar instincts."

" As Roland has tumbled into the mire, better for him to be honest and work," returned Sir Vincent, mincing with his dry toast and one poached egg, for he was delicate in appetite.   " What else could he do ?

Of course there's the credit system and periodical white-washings, but I should not care to go in for that kind of thing myself."

" Are you in want of a bailiff?" growled Gerald, wondering whether the last remarks were meant to be personal.

" Greatorex has engaged one for me. How are you getting on yourself, Gerald ?"

" Not—aw—at all. I'm awfully hard up."

" You always are, Ger, according to your story," was the baronet's remark, laughing slightly.

And somehow the laugh sounded in Gerald's ear as a hard laugh—as one that boded no good results to the petition he meant to prefer before his departure—that Sir Vincent would accommodate him with a loan.

" He's close-fisted as a miser," was Gerald's mental comment. " His father all over again. Neither of them would part with a shilling save for self-gratification : and both could spend enough on *that*. I'll ask him for a hundred, point blank, before I leave ; more, if I can feel my way to do it. Fortune is shamefully unequal in this life. There's Vin with his baronetcy, and his nice little place here and every comfort in it, and his town house, and his clear four thousand a year, and no end of odds and ends of money besides, nest eggs of various shapes and sizes, and his future wife a seventy thousand pounder in her own right; and here's myself by his side, a better man than he any day, with not a coin of my own in the whole world, nor likely to drop into one by inheritance, and afraid to venture about London for fear of being nabbed! Curse the whole thing! He is shabby in trifles too. To give me a miserable two days' invitation. Two days! I'll remain twenty if I can."

"You don't eat, Gerald."

"I've made a famous breakfast, thank you. Do you spend Christmas down here, Vincent?"

"Not I. The day after to-morrow, when you leave me, I start for Paris."

"For Paris!" echoed Gerald, his mouth falling at the sudden failure of his pleasant scheme.

"Miss Trehern and her father are there. We shall remain for the jour de l'an, see the bonbon shops, and all that, and then come back again."

"And I hope the bonbon shops will choke him!" thought kindly Gerald.

Sir Vincent Yorke did not himself go in for keepers and dogs. There was little game on his land, and he was too effeminate to be much of a sportsman. He owned two guns, and that comprised the whole of his shooting paraphernalia. Breakfast over, he had his guns brought, and desired Gerald to take his choice.

Now the handling and understanding of guns did not rank amidst Gerald Yorke's accomplishments. Brought up in the cathedral town, only away from it on occasions at Dr. Yorke's living (and that happened to be in a town also), the young Yorkes were not made familiar with out-door sports. Dr. Yorke had never followed them himself, and saw no necessity for training his sons to them. Even riding they were not very familiar with. Roland's letter has just informed Sir Vincent that he had nearly lost his life *learning to ride* the wild horses when up the country at Port Natal. Probably he had learnt also to understand something about guns : we may be very sure of one thing, that if he did not understand them, he would have voluntarily avowed it. Not so Gerald. Gerald, made up of artificialisms—for nothing seemed real about him but his ill-temper—touched the guns here, and fingered the guns there, and critically examined them everywhere, as if he were the greatest connoisseur alive, and had invented a breech-loader himself ; and finally said he would take *this* one.

So they went out, each with his gun, and

a favourite dog of the baronet's, Spot, and joined a neighbour's shooting party, as had been arranged. Colonel Clutton's land joined Sir Vincent's; he was a keen lover of sport, always making up parties for it, and if Sir Vincent went out at all, it was sure to be with Colonel Clutton.

"To-day and to-morrow will be my last turn-out this season," observed the baronet, as they walked along. "Not sorry for it. One gets a large amount of fatigue: don't think the slaughter compensates for that."

Reaching the meeting-place, they found a party of some three or four gentlemen and two keepers. Gerald was introduced to Colonel Clutton, an elderly man with snow-white hair. The sport set in. It was late in the season, and the birds were getting scarce or wary, but a tolerably fair number fell.

"The gentleman don't seem to handle his gun gainly, sir, as if he'd played with one as a babby," observed one of the keepers confidentially in Sir Vincent's ear.

He alluded to Gerald Yorke. Sir Vincent turned and looked. Though not much addicted to shooting, he was thoroughly conversant with it; and what he saw, as he watched Gerald, a little surprised him.

"I say, Gerald Yorke, you must take care,"

he called out. "Did you never handle a gun before?"

The suggestion offended Gerald: the question nettled him. His face grew dark.

"What do you mean, Sir Vincent?" was his angry answer. He would have liked to affirm his great knowledge of shooting: but his chief practice had been with a pop-gun at school.

Sir Vincent laughed a little. "Don't do any mischief, that's all."

It might have been that the public caution caused Gerald to be more careless, just to prove his proficiency; it might have been that it tended to flurry him. Certainly he would not have caused harm wilfully; but nevertheless it took place.

Not ten minutes after Sir Vincent had spoken, he was crossing a narrow strip of open ground towards a copse. Gerald, leaping through a gap in the hedge not far behind, carrying his gun (like a senseless man) on full cock, contrived, in some inextricable manner, to discharge it. Whether his elbow caught in the leafless branches, or the trigger caught, or what it was, Gerald Yorke never knew, and never will know to his dying day. The charge went off; there was a cry, accompanied by shouts of warning, somebody on the ground in front, and the rest running to surround the fallen man.

" You have no right to come out, sir, unless you can handle a gun properly!" spoke Colonel Clutton to Gerald, in the moment's confusion. " I have been watching your awkwardness all the morning."

Gerald looked pale with fear, dark with anger. He made no reply whatever : only pressed forward to see who was down, the men, in their velveteen coats and leggings, looking much alike. Sir Vincent Yorke.

" It's not much, I think," said the baronet, good-naturedly, as he looked up at Gerald. "But I say, though, you should have candidly answered me that you were not in the habit of shooting, when I sent you the invitation."

No, it was not much. A few shots had entered the calf of the left leg. They got out pocket-handkerchiefs, and tied them tightly round to stop the hemorrhage. The dog, Spot, laid his head close to his master's face, and whined pitiably.

" What sense them dumb animals have !— a'most human !" remarked the keeper.

" This will stop my Paris trip," observed Sir Vincent, as they were conveying him home.

"Better that was stopped than your wedding," replied Colonel Clutton, with a jesting smile. "You keep yourself quiet, now, that you may be well for *that*. Don't talk."

Sir Vincent acquiesced readily. At the best of times he was sensitive to pain, and somewhat of a coward in regard to his own health. At home he was met by a skilful surgeon. The shots were extracted, and Sir Vincent was made comfortable in bed. Gerald Yorke waylaid the doctor afterwards.

"Is it serious? Will he do well? Sir Vincent is my cousin."

"Oh—Mr. Yorke: the gentleman whose gun unfortunately caused the mishap," was the answering remark. "Of course these accidents are always serious, more or less. This one might have been far worse than it is."

"He will do well?"

"Quite well. At least, I hope so. I see nothing to hinder it. Sir Vincent will be a tractable patient, you see; and a good deal lies in that."

"There's no danger, then?"

"Oh no: no danger."

Gerald, relieved on the score of apprehension of consequences, had the grace to express his regret and sorrow to the baronet. Sir

Vincent begged him to think no more about it : only recommended him not to go out with a party in future, until he had had some practice. Gerald, untrue to the end, said he was a little *out* of practice; should soon get into it again. Sir Vincent made quite light of the hurt; it was nothing to speak of, the doctor had said; would not delay his marriage, or anything. But he did not ask Gerald to remain : and that gentleman, in spite of his hints, and his final offer to stay, found he was expected to go. Sir Vincent expressed his acknowledgments, but said he wished for perfect quiet.

So, on the day following the accident, Gerald Yorke returned to town; which was a day sooner than, even at the worst, he had bargained for; and arrived in a temper. Taking one untoward disappointment with another, Gerald's mood could not be expected to be heavenly. He had fully intended to come away with his pockets lined—if by dint of persuasion Sir Vincent could be seduced into doing it. As it was, Gerald had not broached the subject. Sir Vincent was to be kept entirely quiet; and Gerald, with all his native assurance, could not ask a man for money, whom he had just shot.

CHAPTER XXXVII.

PACING his carpet, in the worst state of perturbation possible, was the Reverend Mr. Ollivera. He had so paced it all the morning. Neglecting his ordinary duties, staying indoors when he ought to have been out, unable to eat or to rest, he and his mind were alike in a state of most distressing indecision. The whole of the night had he tossed and turned, and rose up again and again to walk his room, struggling with his conscience. For years past, he had, so to say, *lived* on the anticipation of this hour: when the memory of his dear brother should be cleared of its foul stain, and the true criminal brought to light. And, now that it had come, he was hesitating whether or not to take advantage of it: whether to let the stain remain, and the criminal escape.

Torn to pieces with doubt and pain, was he. Unable to see *where* his duty lay, more than

once, with lifted hands and eyes and heart, a
cry to Heaven to direct him broke from his
lips.   Passages of Scripture, bearing both
ways, crowded on his mind, to puzzle him
the more ; but there was one great lesson he
could not ignore—the loving, merciful teach-
ing of Jesus Christ.

About one o'clock, when the remembrance
of the miserable grave, and of him who had
been so miserably put into it, lay very strong
upon him, Alletha Rye came into the room
with some white cravats of the parson's in
her hand.   She was neat and nice as usual,
wearing a soft merino gown with white-
worked cuffs and collars, her fair hair smooth
and abundant.

"I have done the best I could with them,
sir : cut off the edges and hemmed them
afresh," she said.   "After that, I passed the
iron over them, and they look just as if fresh
got up."

"Thank you," murmured Mr. Ollivera, the
colour flushing his face, and speaking in a
confused kind of manner, like a man overtaken in a crime.

"Great heaven, can I go on with it ?" he
exclaimed, as she went out, leaving the necker-
chiefs on the table.   "Is it possible to believe
that she *did* it ?—with her calm good face,

with her clear honest eye?" he continued in an agony of distress. "Oh, for guidance!— that I may be shown what my course ought to be!"

As a personal matter, to give Alletha Rye into custody would cause him grievous pain. She had lived under the same roof with him, showing him voluntarily a hundred little courtesies and kindnesses. These white cravats of his, just put to rights, had been undertaken in pure good will.

How very much of our terrible seasons of distress might be spared to us, if we could but see a little further than the present moment; than the atmosphere immediately around. Henry William Ollivera might have been saved his: had he but known that while he was doubting, another was acting. Mr. Greatorex had taken it into his own hands, and the house's trouble was, even then, at the very door. In after life, Henry Ollivera never ceased to be thankful that it was not himself who brought it.

A commotion below. Mr. Roland Yorke had entered, and was calling out to the house to bring his dinner. It was taken to him in the shape of some slices of roast mutton and potatoes. When Mrs. Jones had a joint herself, Roland was served from it. That she was no gainer by the bargain, Mrs. Jones was conscious of; the small sum she allowed herself in repayment out of the weekly sovereign, debarred it: but Roland was favoured for the sake of old times.

Close almost upon that, there came a rather quiet double knock at the street door, which Miss Rye went to answer. Roland thought he recognised a voice, and ran out, his mouth full of mutton.

"Why, it's never you, old Butterby! What brings you in London again?"

Whatever brought Mr. Butterby to London, something curious appeared to have brought him to Mrs. Jones's. A policeman had followed him in, and was shutting the street door, with a manner quite at home. There escaped a faint cry from Alletha, and her face turned white as ashes. Roland stared from one to the other.

"What on earth's the matter?" demanded he.

"I'd like to speak to you in private for a minute, Miss Rye," said Mr. Butterby, in a low civil tone. "Tomkins, you wait there."

She went higher up the passage and looked round something like a stag at bay. There was no unoccupied room to take him to. Mr. Brown's frugal dinner tray (luncheon, as he called it) was in his, awaiting his entrance. That the terrible man of law with his officer had come to arrest *him* Alletha never doubted. A hundred wild ideas of telegraphing him some impossible warning, *not* to enter, went teeming through her brain. Tomkins stood on the entrance mat; Roland Yorke, with his accustomed curiosity, put his back against his parlour door-post to watch proceedings.

"Miss Rye, I'd not have done this of my own accord, leastways not so soon, but it has been forced upon me," whispered Mr. Butterby. "I've got to ask you to go with me."

"To ask *me*?" she tremblingly said, while he was showing her a paper: probably the warrant.

"Are you so much surprised: after that there avowal you made to me last night? If I'd gone and told a police officer that *I* had killed somebody, it would not astonish me to be took."

Her face fell. The pallor of her cheeks was coloured by a faint crimson; her eyes flashed with a condemning light.

"I told you in confidence, as one friend might speak to another; in defence of him who was not there to defend himself," she panted. "How could I suppose you would hasten treacherously to use it against me?"

"Ah," said Mr. Butterby, "in things of that sort us law defenders is just the wrong sort to make confidants of. But now, look here, Miss Rye, I didn't go and abuse that confidence, and though it is me that has put the wheels of the law in motion, it is done in obedience to orders, which I had no power to stop. I'm sorry to have to do it: and I've come down with the warrant myself out of respect to you, that things might be accomplished as genteel as might be."

"Now then, Alletha! Do you know that your dinner's getting cold? What on earth are you stopping there for? Who is it?"

The interruption was from Mrs. Jones, called out through the nearly closed door of her parlour. Alletha, making no response, looked fit to die.

"Have you come to arrest me?" she whispered.

"Well, it's about it, Miss Rye. Apprehend, that is. We'll get a cab and you'll go in it with my friend there, all snug and quiet. I'm vexed that young Yorke should just be at home. Tried to get here half an hour earlier, but—"

Mrs. Jones's door was pulled open with a jerk. To describe the aggravated astonishment on her face when she saw the state of affairs, would be a work of skill. Alletha with a countenance of ghastly fear; Mr. Butterby whispering to her; the policeman on the door mat; Roland Yorke looking leisurely on.

"Well, I'm sure!" exclaimed Mrs. Jones. "What may be the meaning of this?"

There could be no evasion now. Had Alletha in her secret heart hoped to keep it from her tart, condemning, and strong-minded sister, the possibility was over. She went down the few steps that led to the room, and entered it; Mr. Butterby close behind her. The latter was shutting the door, when Roland Yorke walked in, taking French leave.

Which of the two stared the most, Mrs. Jones or Roland, and which of the two felt inclined to abuse Mr. Butterby the most, when his errand became known, remains a question to this day. Roland's championship was hot.

"You know you always do take the wrong people, Butterby!"

"Now, young Mr. Yorke, just you concern yourself with your own business, and leave other folks's alone," was the detective's answering reprimand. "I don't see what call you have to be in this here room at all."

In all the phases of the affair, with its attendant conjectures and suspicions, from the first moment that she saw John Ollivera lying dead in her house, the possibility of Alletha's being cognisant of its cause, much less connected with it, had never once entered the head of Mrs. Jones. She stared from one to the other in simple wonder.

"*What* is it you charge my sister with, Butterby?—the death of Counsellor Ollivera?"

"Well, yes; that's it," he answered.

"And how dare you do it?"

"Now, look you here, Mrs. Jones," said Butterby, in a tone of reason, putting his hand calmly on her wrist, "I've told Miss Rye, and I tell you, that these proceedings are instituted by the law, not by me; if I had not come to carry them out, another would, who might have done it in a rougher manner. A woman of your sense ought to see the matter in its right light. I don't say she's guilty, and I hope she'll be able to prove that she's not; but I can tell you this much, Mrs. Jones, there's them that have had their suspicions turned upon her from the first."

Being a woman of sense, as Mr. Butterby delicately insinuated, Mrs. Jones began to feel a trifle staggered. Not at his words: they had little power over *her* mind, but at Alletha's appearance. Leaning against the wall there, white, faint, silent, she looked like one guilty, rather than innocent. And it suddenly struck Mrs. Jones that she did not attempt a syllable in her own defence.

"Why don't you speak out, girl?" she demanded, in her tartest tone. "You can, I suppose?"

But the commotion had begun to cause attention in the quiet house. Not so much from its noise, as by that subtle instinct that makes itself heard, we cannot tell how; and Mr. Ollivera came in.

"Who has done this?" he briefly asked of the detective.

"Mr. Greatorex, sir."

"The next thing they'll do may be to take me up on the charge," spoke Mrs. Jones with acrimony. "What on earth put this into their miserable heads? *You* don't suspect her, I hope, Mr. Ollivera!"

He only looked at Mrs. Jones in silence by way of answer: a grave meaning in his sad face. It spoke volumes: and Mrs. Jones, albeit not one to give way to emotion, or any other kind of weakness, felt as if a jug of cold water were being poured down her back. Straight-forward, always, she put the question to him with naked plainness.

"*Do* you suspect her?"

"I have suspected her," came the low tones of Mr. Ollivera, in answer. "Believe me, Mrs. Jones, whatever may be the final result of this, I grieve for it bitterly."

"I say, why can't you speak up, and say you did not do it?" stamped Roland, in his championship. "Don't be frightened out of your senses by Butterby. He never pitches upon the right person; Mrs. J. remembers *that.*"

"As this here talking won't do any good —and I'm sure if it would I'd let it go on a bit—suppose we make a move," interposed Butterby. "If you'd like to put up a few things to take with you, Miss Rye, do so. You'll have to go to Helstonleigh."

"Oh, law!" cried Roland. "I say, Butterby, it's a mistake, I know. Let her go. Come! you shall have all my dinner."

"Don't stand there like a statue, as if you were moon-struck," said Mrs. Jones, seizing her sister to administer a slight shaking. "Tell them you are innocent, girl, if you can; and let Butterby go about his business."

And in response, Alletha neither spoke nor moved.

But at this moment another actor came upon the scene. A knock at the front door was politely answered at once by the police-man, glad, no doubt, to have something to do, and Mr. Brown entered, arriving at home for his mid-day meal. Roland dashed into the passage.

"I say, Brown, here *is* a stunning shame. Old Butterby's come to take up Alletha Rye."

"Take her up for what ?" Mr. Brown calmly asked.

"For the killing and slaying of Counsellor Ollivera, he says. But in these things he never was anything but a calf."

Mr. Brown turned into his room, put down his hat and a small paper parcel, and went on to the scene. Before he could say a word, Alletha Rye burst forth like one demented.

"Don't come here, Mr. Brown. We've nothing to do with strangers. I can't have all the world looking at me."

Mr. Brown took a quiet survey of matters with perfect self-possession, and then drew Mr. Butterby towards his room, just as though he had possessed the authority of Scotland Yard. Mrs. Jones was left alone with her sister, and caught hold of her two hands.

"Now then ! What is the English of this ?

Had you aught to do with the death of Mr. Ollivera ?"

" Never," said Alletha ; " I would not have hurt a hair of his head."

Mrs. Jones, at the answer, hardly knew whether to slap the young woman's face or to shriek at her. All this disgrace brought upon her house, and Alletha to submit to it in unrefuting tameness ! As a preliminary, she began a torrent of words.

" Hush !" said Alletha. " They think me guilty, and at present they must be let think it. I cannot help myself : if Butterby conveys me to Helstonleigh, he must do it."

Mrs. Jones was nearly staggered out of her passion. The cold water went trickling down again. Not at once could she answer.

" Lord help the wench for a fool ! Don't you know that if you are conveyed to Helstonleigh it would be to take your trial at the next assizes ? Would you face *that* ?"

" I cannot tell," wailed Alletha, putting up her thin hand to her troubled face. " I must have time to think."

But we must follow Mr. Brown. As he passed into his room and closed the door, he took a tolerably long look into Butterby's eyes : possibly hoping to discover whether that astute officer knew him for Godfrey Pitman.

He obtained no result. Had Mr. Butterby been a born natural he could not have looked more charmingly innocent. That he chose to indulge this demand for an interview for purposes of his own, those who knew him could not doubt. They stood together before the fireless hearth; however cold the weather might be, Mr. Brown's fire went out after breakfast and was not re-lighted until night.

"I beg your pardon, Mr. Butterby. With so much confusion in there"—nodding in the direction of Mrs. Jones's parlour—"I am not sure that I fully understood. Is it true that you are about to take Miss Rye into custody on suspicion of having caused the death of John Ollivera?"

"I have took her," was the short answer. "It is nothing to you, I suppose."

"It is this much to me : that I happen to be in a position to testify that she did not do it."

"Oh, you think so, do you," said Butterby, in a civil but slightly mocking tone. "I've knowed ten men at least swear to one man's innocence of a crime, and him guilty all the while. Don't say it was perjury : appearances is deceptive, and human nature's soft."

"I affirm to you, in the hearing of Heaven,

that Alletha Rye was innocent of the death of John Ollivera," said Mr. Brown in a solemn tone that might have carried conviction to even a less experienced ear. "She had nothing whatever to do with it. Until the following morning, when she found him, she was as ignorant as you that he was dead."

"Then why don't she speak up and say so? not that it could make any difference at the present stage of affairs."

"Will you let me ask who it is that has had her apprehended? Mr. Bede Greatorex?"

"Bede Greatorex has had nothing to do with it. 'Twas his father."

"Well now, I have a favour to ask you, Mr. Butterby," continued the other after a pause. "The good name of a young woman is a great deal easier lost than re-gained, as no one can tell better than yourself. It will be an awful thing if Alletha Rye, being innocent —as I swear to you she is—should be accused of this dreadful crime before the world. You have known her a long while : will you not stretch a point to save it?"

"That might depend a good deal upon what the point was," replied Mr. Butterby.

"A very simple one. Only this—that you would stay proceedings until I have had time to see Bede Greatorex. Let her remain here, in custody of course—for I am not so foolish as to suppose you could release her—but don't molest her; don't take her away. In fact, *treat her as though you knew* she were wrongfully accused. You may be obliged to me for this later, Mr. Butterby—I won't say in the interests of humanity, but of justice."

Various thoughts and experiences of the past, as connected with Bede Greatorex, came crowding into the mind of Butterby. His lips parted with a smile, but it was not a favourable one.

"I think that Bede Greatorex could join with me in satisfying you that it was not Miss Rye," urged the petitioner. "I am almost sure he can do this if he will."

"Which is as much as to say that both he and you have got your suspicions turned on some other quarter," rejoined Butterby. "Who was it?"

That Mr. Brown's cheeks took a darker tinge at the direct query, was plain to be seen. He made no answer.

"Come! Who did that thing? *You* know."

"If I do not know—and I am unable to tell you that I do, Mr. Butterby—I can yet make a shrewd guess at it."

"And Bede Greatorex too, you say?"

"I fancy he can."

Looking into each other's eyes, those two deep men, there ensued a silence. "If it wasn't this woman," whispered Butterby, "perhaps it was another."

The clerk opened his lips to speak in hasty impulse: but he closed them again, still looking hard at the officer.

"Whether it was or not, the woman was not Alletha Rye."

"Then," said Mr. Butterby, following out his own private thoughts, and giving the table an emphatic slap, which caused the frugal luncheon tray to jingle, "this thing will never be brought to trial."

"I don't much think it will," was the significant answer. "But you will consent to what I ask? I won't be away long. A quarter of an hour will suffice for my interview with Bede Greatorex."

Weighing chances and possibilities, as it lay in the business of Mr. Butterby to do; knowing who the man before him was, with the suspicion attaching to him, he thought it might be as well to keep him under view. There was no apparent intention to escape; the clerk seemed honest as the day on this present purpose, and strangely earnest; but

Mr. Butterby had learnt to trust nobody.

"I'll go with you," said he. "Tomkins will
keep matters safe here. Come on. Hang
me if this case ever had its fellow: it turns
one about with its little finger."

CHAPTER XXXVIII.

They stood near each other, Bede Greatorex and his managing clerk, while Mr. Butterby paced the passage outside.

When interrupted, Bede had his elbow on the mantle-piece, his brow bent on his thin fingers. A good blazing fire here, the coal crackling and sparkling cheerily. Bede dropped his elbow.

"What is it, Mr. Brown?" he rather languidly asked.

Mr. Brown, closing the door, went straight up and said what it was: Alletha Rye had been apprehended. But he looked anywhere, as he spoke, rather than into the face of his master. A face that grew suddenly white and cold: and Mr. Brown, in his delicacy of mind, would not appear to see it.

"What a cursed meddler that Butterby is!" exclaimed Bede.

12—2

"I fancy he had no option in this, sir; that it was not left to his choice."

"Who did it, then?"

"Mr. Greatorex. This must be remedied at once, sir."

By the authoritative manner in which he spoke, it might have been thought that Bede Greatorex was the servant, Brown the master. Bede put his elbow on the shelf again, and pushed back his hair in unmistakable agitation. It was growing thin now, the once luxuriant crop; and silver threads were interwoven with the black ones.

"She must be saved," repeated Mr. Brown.

"I suppose so. Who is to do it?"

"I must, sir. If no one else does."

Bede raised his eyes to glance at his clerk; but it was not a full free glance, and they were instantly dropped again.

"You are the Godfrey Pitman, they tell me, who was in the house at the time."

"Yes, I am. But have you not known it all along, Mr. Bede Greatorex?"

"All along from when?"

Mr. Brown hesitated. "From the time that I came here as clerk."

"No; certainly I have not."

"There were times, sir, when I fancied it."

A long silence. Even now, whatever secret, or association, there might be between these two men, neither was at ease with the other. Bede especially seemed to shrink from further explanation.

"I have known but for a short while of your identity with Godfrey Pitman," he resumed. "And with George Winter. I have been waiting my own time to confer with you upon the subject. We have been very busy."

We have been very busy! If Bede put that forth as an excuse, it did not serve him: for his hearer knew it was not the true one. He simply answered that they *had* been very busy. Not by so much as a look or a syllable would George Winter—let us at last give him his true name—add to the terrible pain he knew his master must be suffering.

"About Miss Rye, sir? She must be extricated from her unpleasant position."

"Yes, of course."

"And her innocence proved."

"At the expense of another?" asked Bede, without lifting his eyes.

"No," answered the other in a low tone. "I do not think that need be."

Bede looked straight into the fire, his companion full at the window-blind, drawn half way down ; neither of them at one another.

"How will you avoid it ?" asked Bede.

"I think it may be avoided, sir. For a little while past, I have foreseen that some such a crisis as this would come : and I have dwelt and dwelt upon it until I seem to be able to track out my way in it perfectly clear."

Bede cracked the coal in the grate ; which did not require cracking. "Do you mean that you have foreseen Miss Rye would be taken ? Such a thought in regard to her never crossed my mind."

"Nor mine. I alluded to myself, sir. If once I was discovered to be the so-called Godfrey Pitman—and some instinct told me the discovery was at last approaching—I knew that I should, in all probability, be charged with the murder of Mr. Ollivera. I —an innocent man—would not suffer for this, Mr. Greatorex ; I should be obliged, in self-defence, to repel the accusation : and I have been considering how it might be done without compromising others. I think it can be."

"How ?" repeated Bede shortly.

"By my not telling the whole truth. By not knowing—I mean not having recognised the—the one—who would be compromised if I did tell it. I think this is feasible, sir."

Just a momentary glance into each other's eyes ; no more ; and it spoke volumes. Bede, facing the fire again, stood several minutes in deep consideration. George Winter seemed occupied with one of his gloves that had a refractory button.

" In any case it must now be known who you are," said Bede.

" That will not signify. In throwing the onus of the——" he seemed to hesitate, as he had once hesitated in the last sentence —" the death off Miss Rye, I throw it equally off my own shoulders. I have for some months wished that I could declare myself."

" Why have you not done it ?"

George Winter looked at his master, sur- prise in his eyes. " It is not for my own sake that I have kept concealed, sir."

No. Bede Greatorex knew that it was for *his;* at least for his interests ; and felt the obligation in his heart. He did not speak it ; pride and a variety of other unhappy feelings kept him silent. Of all the miserable mo- ments that the death of John Ollivera had entailed upon him, this confidential interview with his clerk was not the least of them. Forced though he was to hold it, he hated it with his whole soul.

" You took that cheque from my desk,"

said Bede. "And wrote me the subsequent letter."

"I did not take it from the desk, sir. Your expressed and continuous belief—that you had put it in—was a mistaken one. It must have slipped from your hands when about to lock up the other papers you held, and fluttered under the desk-table. Perhaps you will allow me to give you the explanation now."

Bede nodded.

"In the morning of the day that the cheque was lost, you may remember coming into the front room and seeing a stranger with me. His name was Foster; a farmer and corn-dealer near Birmingham. I had been out on an errand; and, on turning in again, a gentleman stopped me to enquire the way. While I was directing him there ensued a mutual recognition. In one sense I owed him some money: forty-four pounds. Samuel Teague, of whom you may have heard——"

"I know," interrupted Bede.

"Samuel Teague, just before he ran away, had got me to put my name to a bill for him; Mr. Foster, in all good faith, had let him have the money for it. It had never been repaid. But upon Mr. Foster's meeting me that morning, he gave me my choice—to find the money for him before he left London, or be denounced publicly as George Winter.   I thought he would have denounced me then.   He came into the office and would not be got rid of: saying that he had looked for me too long to let me go, now that I was found.   What I was to do I did not know.   *I* had no objection to resume my own name, for I had cleared myself with Johnson and Teague, but it must have involved the exposure relating to the affair at Helstonleigh.   The thought occurred to me of declaring the dilemma to you, letting you decide whether that exposure should come, or whether you would lend me the forty-four pounds to avert it.   But I shrank from doing that."

"Why?" again interposed Bede.

"Because I thought *you* would dislike my entering upon the subject, sir.   I have shrunk from it always.   Now that the necessity is forced upon me, I am shrinking from it as I speak."

Ah, but not so much as Bede was.   "Go on."

"While I sat at my desk, inwardly deliberating, Mr. Frank came in, asking you to draw out a cheque for Sir Richard Yorke for forty-four pounds.   The strange coincidence between the sum and the money demanded

of me, struck me as being most singular. It
strikes me so still. Later in the morning, I
came into this room with some deeds, and
saw a piece of paper lying under the table.
Upon picking it up—which I did simply to
replace it on the desk—I found it was the
cheque. My first thought was that it must
be a special, almost a supernatural, interven-
tion in my favour; my second, that it was
just possible you had left it there for me to
take. Both ideas very far-fetched and imagi-
natory, as I saw at once. But I used the
cheque, Mr. Bede Greatorex. I went home,
put on the false hair I had worn as Godfrey
Pitman, for I have it by me still, and got the
cheque cashed in gold. It was not for my
sake I did this; I hated it bitterly. And
then I hesitated to use the money. At night
I went to Mr. Foster's hotel, and told him
that I would get the money for him by the
following night *if I could*; if I could not, he
must carry out his threat of denouncing me
to the public and Mr. Greatorex. Foster con-
sented to wait. I returned to my lodgings
and wrote that anonymous note to you, sir,
not telling you who had taken the cheque;
merely saying that exposure was threatened
of the private circumstances, known only to
one or two, attendant on Mr. Ollivera's death

at Helstonleigh ; that the money had been taken to avert the exposure, and would be applied to that purpose, provided you were agreeable.   If not, and you wished the money returned, you were requested to drop a note without loss of a moment to a certain address : if no such note were written, the money would be used in the course of the day, and things kept silent as heretofore.   You sent no answer, and I paid it to Foster in the evening.   I have never been able to decide whether you suspected me as the writer, or not."

"No.   I fancied it might be Hurst."

"Hurst!" exclaimed George Winter in great surprise.

Bede looked up for a moment.   "I felt sure the cheque must have been taken by one of you in the next room.   Not knowing you then for Godfrey Pitman, my thoughts fell on Hurst.   His father was the attendant surgeon, and might have made some critical discovery."

"I don't see how he could have done that, sir," was the dissenting answer.

"Nor did I.   But it is the doubt in these cases that causes the fear.   I should like to ask you a question—was it by accident or purposed design that you came to our house as a clerk ?"

"Purely by accident.   When the misfortunes fell upon me in Birmingham, and I was unwise enough to follow Samuel Teague's example and run away, I retained one friend, who stood by me. After quitting Helstonleigh on the Monday night, I concealed myself elsewhere for three or four days, and then went to him in Essex, where he lived. He procured me a clerkship in a lawyer's office in the same county, Mr. Cale's, with whom I stayed about a year. Mr. Cale found me very useful, and when his health failed, and he retired in consequence from practice, he sent me up here to Mr. Greatorex with a strong recommendation."

"You have served us well," said Bede. "Was not your quitting Birmingham a mistake?"

"The worst I ever made. I solemnly declare that I was entirely innocent. Not only innocent myself, but unsuspicious of anything wrong on the part of Samuel Teague. He took me in, as he took in everybody else. Johnson and Teague know it now, and have at length done me the justice to acknowledge it. I knew of young Teague's profuse expenditure : he used to tell me he had the money from his uncle, old Mr. Teague, and it never occurred to me to doubt it. Where I erred, was in going to the old man and blurting out the truth. He died of the shock. I shall never forgive myself for that : it seemed to me always as though I had murdered him. With his dead form, as it seemed, pursuing me, with the knowledge that I was to be included in the charge of forgery, I lost my sober senses.   In my fright, I saw no escape but in flight; and I got away on the Sunday afternoon as far as Helstonleigh.   It was in the opposite direction to the one Samuel Teague was thought to have taken, and I wanted to see Alletha Rye, if it were practicable, and assure her before we finally parted, that, though bad enough, I was not quite the villain people were making me out to be. There—there are strange coincidences in this life, Mr. Bede Greatorex."

"You may well say that," answered Bede.

"And one of the strangest was that of my accidentally meeting Alletha Rye five minutes after I reached Helstonleigh.   Forgetting my disguise, I stopped to accost her—and have not forgotten her surprise yet.   But I had not courage then to tell her the truth : I simply said I was in trouble through false friends, and was ill—which was really the case—and I asked her if she could shelter me for a day or two, or could recommend me to a place where I might be private and to myself. The result was, that I went to Mrs. Jones's house, introduced as a stranger, one Godfrey Pitman. I hit upon the name hap-hazard. And before I left it I was drawn into that business concerning Mr. Ollivera."

Bede Greatorex made no answer. A coincidence! Aye; one of heaven's sending.

"Why so much ill-luck should have fallen upon me I cannot tell," resumed George Winter. "I started in life, hoping and intending to do my duty as conscientiously as most men do it; and I've tried to, that's more. Fate has not been kind to me."

"There are others that it has been less kind to," spoke Bede, his tone marked with ill-suppressed agitation. "Your liabilities in Birmingham? Are they wiped out?"

"Others' liabilities you mean, sir; I had none of my own. Yes, I have scraped, and saved, and paid; paid all. I am saving now to repay *you* the forty-four pounds, and have about twenty towards it. But for having my good old mother on my hands—she lives in Wales—I should have been clear earlier."

"You need not trouble yourself about the forty-four pounds," said Bede, recognising the wondrous obligations he and his were under to this silent, self-denying man.

"If it were forty-four hundred, sir, I should work on until I paid it, life being granted me."

"Very well," replied Bede. "I may be able to recompense you in another way."

If Bede Greatorex thought that any simple order of his would release Miss Rye from custody, he found himself mistaken. Butterby, called into the conference, was almost pleasantly derisive.

"You'll assure me she was not guilty! and Mr. Brown there can assure me she was not guilty! And, following them words up, you say, 'Let her go, Butterby!' Why, you might about as well tell me to let the stars drop out of the sky, Mr. Bede Greatorex. I've no more power over one than I have over the other."

"But she is innocent," reiterated Bede. "Mr. Brown here—you know who he is—can testify to it."

Butterby gave a careless nod in the direction of Mr. Brown—as much as to say that his knowing who he was went for a matter of course. But he was sternly uncompromising.

"Look here, Mr. Bede Greatorex. It's all very well for you to say to me, Miss Rye's innocent; and for that there clever gentleman by your side to say she's innocent—and himself too, I suppose he'd like to add; but you, as a lawyer, must know that all that is of no manner of use. If you two will bring forward the right party, and say, 'This is the one that was guilty,' and *prove* it to the satisfaction of the law and Mr. Greatorex, that would be another thing. Only in that case can Miss Rye be set at liberty."

"You—you do not know what family interests are involved in this, Mr. Butterby," Bede said in a tone of pain.

"Can guess at 'em," responded Butterby.

Bede inwardly thought the boast was a mistaken one, but he let it pass.

"If my father were acquainted with the true facts of the case," spoke he, "he would never bring it to a public trial; I tell you this on my honour."

"You know yourself who the party was; I see that," said Butterby.

"I do—Heaven spare me!"

There was a strange tone of helplessness mingling with the anguish of the avowal, as if Bede could contend with fate no longer. Even the officer felt for him. George Winter looked round at him with a glance of caution, as much as to say there was no necessity to avow too much. Bede bent his head, and strove to see, as well as the hour's trouble and perplexity would allow him, what might and what might not be done. Butterby, responsible to the magistrates at Helstonleigh who had granted the warrant, would have to be satisfied, as well as Mr. Greatorex.

Another minute, and Bede went forth to seek an interview with his father, who was alone in his room. Bede, almost as though he were afraid of his courage leaving him, entered upon the matter before he had well closed the door. Not in any torrent of words: he spoke but a few, and those with almost painful calmness : but his breath was laboured, himself perceptibly agitated.

"Give my authority to Butterby to release Alletha Rye from custody, because you happen to know that she is innocent!" exclaimed Mr. Greatorex in surprise. "Why, what can you mean, Bede ?"

Bede told his tale. Hampered by various doubting fears lest he might drop an unsafe word, it was rather a lame one. Mr. Greatorex leaned back in his chair, and looked up at Bede as he listened. They held, unconsciously, much the same position as they had that March day nearly five years ago in another room, when the tale of the death was first told, Bede having then just got up with it from Helstonleigh : Mr. Greatorex sitting, Bede standing with his arm on the mantlepiece, his face partly turned away. Bede had grown quite into the habit of standing thus, to press his hand on his brow : it seemed as though some weight or pain were always there.

"I don't understand you, Bede," spoke Mr. Greatorex frankly. "You tell me that you know of your own cognisance Alletha Rye was innocent ? That you knew it at the time ?"

"Almost of my own cognisance," corrected Bede.

"Which must be equivalent to saying that you know who was guilty."

"No ; I—don't know that," murmured Bede, his face growing damp with the conscious lie.

"Then what do you know, that you should wish to interfere ? You have always said it was a case of suicide."

"It was not that, father," was Bede's low, shrinking answer. But he looked into his father's eyes with thrilling earnestness as he gave it.

Mr. Greatorex began to feel slightly uncomfortable. He detested mystery of all kinds ; and there was something unpleasantly mysterious in Bede's voice and looks and words and manner.

"Did you know at the time that it was not suicide ?" pursued Mr. Greatorex.

How should Bede get through this? say what he must say, and yet not say too much? He inwardly asked himself the question.

"There was just a suspicion of it on my mind, sir. Any way, Alletha Rye must be set at liberty."

"I do not understand what you say, Bede; I do not understand *you*. Your manner on this subject has always been an enigma. William Ollivera holds the opinion that you must be screening some one."

A terrible temptation, hard to battle with, assailed Bede Greatorex at the charge—to avow to his father who and what he had been screening ever since the death. He forced himself to silence until it had passed.

"What is troubling you, Bede?"

Mr. Greatorex might well ask it; with that sad countenance in front of him, working with its pain. In his grievous perplexity, Bede gave the true answer.

"I was thinking if it were possible for Pitman's explanation to be avoided, father."

"What! Is Pitman found?"

"Yes, he is found," quietly answered Bede. "He——"

The room door was opening to admit some visitors, and Bede turned. Surely the propitious star to the House of Greatorex could not be in the ascendant ! For they were Judge Kene and Henry William Ollivera.

And the concealment that he had striven and toiled for, and worn out his health and life to keep ; fighting ever, mentally or bodily, against Fate's relentless hand, was felt to be at an end by Bede Greatorex.

CHAPTER XXXIX.

On a sofa, drawn at right angles with the fire, lay Hamish Channing; his bright head raised high, a crimson coverlid of eider down thrown over his feet. In the last day or two he had grown perceptibly worse; that is, weaker. The most sanguine amidst his friends, medical or others, could not say there was hope now. But, as long as he could keep up, Hamish would not give in to his illness: he rose in the morning and made a pretence of going about the house; and when he was tired, lay on the sofa that had been put into his writing-room. It was the room he felt most at home in, and he seemed to cling to it.

On the other side the hearth, bending forward in his chair, staring at Hamish with sad eyes, and pulling at his whiskers in grievous gloom, sat Roland Yorke. Roland had abandoned his home-copying for the past two days, and spent all his spare time with Hamish.

Mrs. Jones, snatching a moment to go and visit Mr. Channing for old association's sake, had been very much struck with what she saw in him, and carried home the news that he was certainly dying. Roland, believing Mrs. J. to be as correct in judgment as she was tart in speech, had been looking out for death from that moment. Previously he was given to waver; one moment in despair; the next, up in the skies with exultation and thinking recovery had set in. The wind could not be more variable than Roland.

It was the twilight hour of the winter's day. The room was not lighted yet, but the blaze from the fire played on Hamish's face as he lay. There was a change in it to-night, and it told upon Roland : for it looked like the shadow of death. Things seemed to have been rather at sixes and sevens in the office that afternoon : Mr. Brown was absent, Hurst had gone home for Christmas, Bede Greatorex did not show himself, and there was nobody to tell Roland what work to be about. Of course it presented to that gentleman's mind a most valuable opportunity for enjoying a spell of recreation, and he took French leave to abandon it to itself and little Jenner. Rushing home in the first place, to see what might be doing there—for it was the day that Miss Rye had been captured by Butterby. Roland had his run for his pains. There was nothing doing, and his curiosity and good nature alike suffered. Miss Rye was a prisoner still; she, and Mrs. Jones, and the policeman left in charge, being shut up in the parlour together. "It's an awful shame of old Butterby!" cried Roland, to himself, as he sped along to Hamish's. There he took up his station in his favourite chair, and watched the face that was fading so rapidly away. With an etherealized look in it that spoke of heaven, with a placid calm that seemed to partake of the fast approaching rest; with a sweet smile that told of altogether inward peace, there the face lay; and Roland thought he had never seen one on earth so like an angel's.

Hamish had dropped into a doze; as he often did, at the close of day, when darkness is silently spreading over the light. Nelly Channing, who had learnt—by that subtle warning that sometimes steals, we know not how, over the instinct of little ones about to be made orphans—that some great and sad change was looming in the air, sat on a stool on the hearth-rug as sedately as any old woman. Nelly's boisterous ways and gleeful

laugh had left her for a while : example perhaps taught her to be still, and she largely
profited by it.

On her lap lay a story book : papa had
bought it for her yesterday : that is, had given
the money to Miss Nelly and nurse when
they went out, and wrote down the title of
the book they were to buy, and the shop they
might get it at, with his own trembling fingers,
out of which the strength had nearly gone.
It was one of those exquisite story books that
ought to be in all children's hands, Mrs. Sher-
wood's ; belonging of course to a past day, but
nothing has since been written like them.

With every leaf that she silently turned,
Nelly looked to see that it did not wake the
invalid. When she grew tired, and her face
was roasted to a red heat, she went to Roland,
resting the open book upon his knee. He
lifted her up.

" It is such a pretty book, Roland."

" All right. Don't you make a noise,
Nelly."

" Margaret went to heaven in the book :
she was buried under the great yew tree,"
whispered Nelly. " Papa's going there."

Roland caught the little head to him, and
bent his face on the golden hair. He knew
that what she said was true : but it was a

shock nevertheless to have it repeated openly to him even by this young child.

" Papa talks to me about it. It will be so beautiful ; he will never be tired there, or have any sorrow or pain. Oh, Roland ; I wish I was going with him !"

Her eyes were filled with tears as she looked up ; Roland's were filled in sympathy. He had cried like a schoolboy more than once of late. All on a sudden, happening to glance across, he saw Hamish looking on with a smile.

" You be off, Nelly," said arbitrary Roland, carrying her to the door and shutting it upon her and her book. " I'm sure your tea must be ready in the nursery."

" Don't grieve, Roland," said Hamish, when he sat down again.

" I wish you could get well," returned Roland, seeing the fire through a mist.

" And I have nearly ceased to wish it, Roland. It's all for the best."

" Ceased to wish it ! How's that ?"

" Through God's mercy, I think."

The words silenced Roland. When anything of this kind was mentioned it turned him into a child, so far as his feelings went ; simple as Miss Nelly, was he, and a vast deal more humble-minded.

"Things are being cleared for me so wonderfully, Roland. But for leaving some who are dear to me, the pain would be over."

"I wish I could come across that fiend who wrote the reviews!" was Roland's muttered answer to this. "I *wish* I could!"

"What?" said Hamish, not catching the words.

"I *will* say it, then; I don't care," cried impetuous Roland—for no one had ever spoken before Hamish of what was supposed to have caused him the cruel pain. Roland blurted it all out now in his explosive fashion; his own long-suppressed wrath, and what he held in store for the anonymous reviewer, when he should have the good fortune to come across him.

A minute's silence when he ceased, a wild hectic spreading itself into the hollow cheeks —that it should so stir him even yet! Hamish held out his hand, and Roland came across to take it. The good sweet eyes looked into his.

"If ever you do 'come across' him, Roland, say that I forgive," came the low, earnest whisper. "I did think it cruel at the time; well nigh too hard to bear; but, like most other crosses, I seem to see now that it came to me direct from heaven."

" That *is* good, Hamish !   Come !"

" We must through much tribulation enter into the kingdom," whispered Hamish, looking up at him with a yearning smile.   " You have in all probability a long life before you, Roland : but the time may come when you will realise the truth of those words."

Roland swallowed down a lump in his throat as he turned to the fire again.   Hamish resumed, changing his tone for one almost of gaiety.

" I have had good news to-day.   Our friend the publisher called ; and what do you think he told me, Roland ?   That my book was finding its way at last."

" Of course it will.   Everybody always thought it must.   If you could but have put off for a time your bother over the reviews, Hamish !" Roland added piteously.

" Ay.   He says that in three months' time from this, the book will be in every one's hands.   In the satisfaction of the news, I sat down and eat some luncheon with him and Ellen."

" Don't you think the news might be enough to cure you ?" asked sanguine Roland.

Hamish shook his head.   " If I were able to feel joy now as I felt the sorrow, it might perhaps go a little way towards it. But that is over, Roland. The capability of feeling either in any degree was crushed out of me."

Roland rubbed up his hair. If he had but that enemy of his under his hand, and a spacious arena that admitted of pitching-in!

"And now for some more good news, Roland. You must know how I have been troubled at the thought of leaving Ellen and the child unprovided for—"

"I say, *don't* you! Don't you trouble, Hamish," came the impulsive interruption. "I'll work for them. I'll do my very best for them, as well as for Annabel."

"It won't be needed, dear old friend," and Hamish's face, with its bright, grateful smile, almost looked like the sunny one of old. "Ellen's father, Mr. Huntley, is regaining the wealth he feared he had lost. As an earnest of it, he has sent Ellen two hundred pounds. It was paid her to-day."

"Oh, now, isn't that good, Hamish!"

"Very good!" answered Hamish, reverently and softly, as certain words ran through his mind: 'So great is His mercy towards them that trust in Him.' "And so, Roland, all things are working round pleasantly that I may die in peace."

Mrs. Channing, coming in with her things

on, for she had been out on some necessary business, interrupted the conversation. She mentioned to Roland that she had seen Gerald drive up to his wife's rooms, and that he had promised to come round.

"Why I thought he was at Sunny Mead with Dick!"

"He told me he had just returned from it," said Mrs. Channing.

"I say, Hamish, who knows but he may have brought me up a message!" cried Roland.

Hamish smiled. Roland had disclosed the fact in family conclave, of his having applied for the place of bailiff to Sir Vincent; Annabel being present. He had recited, so far as he could remember them, the very words of the letter, over which Hamish had laughed himself into a coughing-fit.

"To be sure," answered Hamish, with a touch of his old jesting spirit. "Gerald may have brought up your appointment, Roland."

That was quite enough. "I'll go and ask him," said Roland eagerly. "Any way he may be able to tell me how Dick received it."

Away went Roland, on the spur of the moment. It was a clear, cold evening, the air sharp and frosty ; and Roland ran all the way to Mrs. Gerald Yorke's.

That lady was not in tears this evening; but her mood was a gloomy one, her face fractious. The tea was on the table, and she was cutting thick bread-and-butter for the three little girls sitting so quietly round it, before their cups of milk-and-water. Gerald had gone out again ; she did not know where, whether temporarily, or to his chamber for the night, or anything about him.

"I think something must have gone wrong at Sunny Mead," observed Winny. "When I asked what brought him back so soon, he only swore. Perhaps Sir Vincent refused to lend money, and they had a quarrel. I know Gerald meant to ask him : he is in dreadful embarrassment."

"Mamma," pleaded a little voice, "there's no butter on my bread."

"There's as much as I can afford to put, Kitty," was Mrs. Yorke's answer. "I must keep some for the morning. Suppose your papa should find no butter for breakfast, if he comes home to sleep to-night! My goodness !"

"Bread and scrape's not good, is it Kitty ?" said Roland.

"No," plaintively answered the child.

Roland clattered out, taking the stairs at a leap. Mrs. Yorke supposed he had left without the ceremony of saying good-night.

"Just like his manners!" she fractiously cried. "But oh! don't I wish Gerald was like him in temper!"

Roland had not gone for the night. He happened to have a shilling in his pocket, and went to buy a sixpenny pot of marmalade. As he was skimming back with it, his eye fell on some small shrimps, exposed for sale on a fishmonger's board. The temptation (with the loose sixpence in his hand) was not to be resisted.

He carried in the treasures. But that the three little ones were very meek spirited, they would have shouted at the sight. Roland lavishly spread the marmalade on the bread-and-scrape, and began pulling out shrimps for the company round, while he talked of Hamish.

"They are saying that those reviews that were so harsh upon his book, have helped to kill him," said Mrs. Yorke, in a low tone, turning from the table to face Roland.

"But for those reviews he'd not have died," answered Roland. "I never will believe it. Illness might have come on, but he'd have had the spirit to throw it off again."

"Yes. When I sit and look at him, Roland, it seems as if I and Gerald were wretches that ought to hide ourselves. I say to myself, it was not my fault; but I *feel* it for all that."

"Why what do you mean?" asked Roland.

"About the reviews. I can't bear to go there now."

"What about the reviews?"

"It was Gerald who wrote them."

Roland, for convenience sake, had the plate of shrimps on his knee during the picking process. He rested from his work and stared in a kind of puzzle. Winny continued.

"Those reviews were all Gerald's doings. That dreadful one in the *Snarler* he wrote himself, here, and was two days over it, getting to it at times as ideas and strong words occurred to him to make it worse and worse—just as, he wrote the one of praise on his own book. The other reviews, that were every bit as bad, he got written. I read every word of the one in the *Snarler* in manuscript. I wanted to tell him it was wicked, but he might have shaken me. He said he owed Hamish Channing a grudge, and should get his book damned. That's not my word, you know, Roland. And, all the while, it was Hamish who was doing so much for me and the poor children ; finding us in food when Gerald did not."

No whiter could Hamish Channing's face look when the marble paleness of death should have overshadowed it, than Roland's was now. For a short while it seemed as though the communication were too astounding to find admittance to his mind. Suddenly he rose up with a great cry. Down went shrimps, and plate, and all ; and he was standing upright before Mrs. Yorke.

"Is it true ? Is it *true* ?"

"Why of course it's true," she fractiously answered, for the movement had startled her. "Gerald did it all. I'd not tell anybody but you, Roland."

Throwing his hat on his head, hind part before, away dashed Roland. Panting, wild, his breath escaping him in great sobs, like unto one who has received some strong mental shock, he arrived at Mr. Channing's in a frantic state. Vague ideas of praying at Hamish's feet for forgiveness, were surging through his brain—for it seemed to Roland that *he*, as Gerald's brother, must be in a degree responsible for this terrible thing.

The door opened, he turned into the dining-room, and found himself in the presence of— Gerald. Hamish, feeling unusually weak, had gone up to bed, and Gerald was waiting the signal to go to him. As he supposed he must call to see Hamish before it should be too late—for Ellen had told him how it was, that afternoon—he had come at once to get the visit over.

Of all the torrents of reproach ever flung at a man, Gerald found himself astounded by about the worst. It was not loud ; loudness might have carried off somewhat of the sting ; but painfully sad and bitter. Roland stood on the hearth-rug in front of Gerald as he had but now stood before Gerald's wife ; with the same white and stricken face ; with the same agitation shaking him from head to foot. The sobbing words broke from him in jerks ; the voice was a wail.

"Was it not enough that I brought disgrace on Arthur Channing in the years gone by, but you, another of us ill-doing Yorkes, must destroy Hamish?" panted Roland. "Good Lord ! why did heaven suffer us two to live ! As true as we are standing together here, Gerald, had I known at the time those false reviews were yours, I should have broken your bones for you.

"You shut up," retorted Gerald. "It's nothing to you."

"Nothing to me ! Nothing to *me*—when

one of the best men that ever lived on earth has been wilfully sent to his grave ? Yes ; I don't care how you may salve-over your conscience, Gerald Yorke ; it is murder, and nothing less. What had he done to you ? He was a true friend, a true, good friend to you and to me : what crime against us had he committed, that you should treat him like this ?"

"If you don't go out of the house, I will," said Gerald. But Roland never seemed to so much as hear it.

"Who do you suppose has been helping you all this year ?" demanded Roland. "When you were afraid of the county-court over a boot bill, somebody paid the money and sent you the receipt anonymously : who has kept your wife and children in rent and clothes and food and all kinds of comforts, while you gave wine parties in your chambers, and went starring it over the seas for weeks in people's yachts ? Hamish Channing. He deprived himself of his holiday, that your wife and children might be fed, you abandoning them : he has lived sparingly in spite of his failing health, that you and yours might profit. You and he were brought up in the same place, boys together, and he could not see your children want. They've never had a fraction of help but what it came from Hamish and his wife."

"It is a lie," said Gerald. But he was staggered, and he half felt that it was not.

"It is the truth, as heaven knows," cried Roland, breaking down with a burst. "Ask Winny, *she* told me. I'd have given my own poor worthless life freely, to save the pain of those false and cruel reviews to Hamish."

Sheer emotion stopped Roland's tongue. Mrs. Channing, entering, found the room in silence; the storm was over. Roland escaped. Gerald, amazingly uncomfortable, had a mind to run away there and then.

"Will you come up, Gerald?" she said.

Hamish lay in bed in his large cheerful chamber, bright with fire and light. His head was raised; one hand was thrown over the white coverlid; and a cup of tea waited on a stand by the bed-side. Roland stood by the fire, his chest heaving.

"But what is it, old fellow?" demanded Hamish. "What has put you out?"

"It is *this*, Hamish—that I wish I could have died instead of you," came the answer at last, with a burst of grief.

He sat down in the shade in a quiet corner, for his brother's step was heard. As Gerald approached the bed, he visibly recoiled. It was some time since he had seen Hamish, and he verily believed he stood in the presence of death. Hamish held out his hand with a cheering smile, and his face grew bright.

"Dear old friend! I thought you were never coming to see me."

Gerald Yorke was not wholly bad, not quite devoid of feeling. With the dying man before him, with the truths he had just heard beating their refrain in his ears, he nearly broke down as Roland had done. Oh, that he could undo his work! that he could recall life to the fading spirit as easily as he had done his best to take it away! These regrets always come rather late, Mr. Gerald Yorke.

"I did not think you were so ill as this, Hamish. Can nothing be done?"

"Don't let it grieve you, Gerald. Our turns must all come, sooner or later. Don't, old fellow," he added in a whisper. "I must keep up for Ellen's sake. God is helping me to do it : oh, so wonderfully."

Gerald bent over him : he thought they were alone. "Will you forgive me?"

"Forgive you!" repeated Hamish, not understanding what there was to forgive.

And Gerald, striving against his miserably

pricking conscience, could not bring himself to say. No, though it had been to save his own life, he dared not confess to his cowardly sin.

"I have not always been the good friend to you I might, Hamish. Do say you forgive me, for Heaven's sake!"

Hamish took his hand, a sweet smile upon his face. "If there is anything you want my forgiveness for, Gerald, take it. Take it freely. Oh Gerald, when we begin to realize the great fact that our sins are forgiven, forgiven and washed out, you cannot think how *glad* we are to forgive others who may have offended us. But I don't know what I have to forgive in you."

Gerald's chest heaved. Roland's, in his distant chair in the shade, heaved rebelliously.

"I had ambitious views for you, Gerald. I meant to do you good if I could. I thought when my book was out and had brought funds to me, I would put you straight. I was so foolishly sanguine as to fancy the returns would be large. I thought of you nearly as much as I thought of myself: one of my dear old friends of dear old Helstonleigh. The world is fading from me, Gerald; but the old scenes and times will be with me to the last. Yes, I had hoped to benefit you, Gerald, but it was otherwise ordained. God bless you, dear friend. God love and prosper you, and bring you home to Him !"

Gerald could not stand it any longer. As he left the room and the house, Roland went up to the bed with a burst, and confessed all. To have kept in the secret would have choked him.

Gerald was the enemy who had done it all ; Gerald Yorke had been the one to sow the tares amid the wheat in his neighbour's field.

A moment of exquisite pain for Hamish ; a slight, short struggle with the human passions, not yet quite dead within his aching breast; and then his loving kindness resumed its sway, never again to quit him.

" Bring him back to me, dear Roland; bring him back that I may send him on his way with words of better comfort," he whispered, with his ineffable smile of peace.

CHAPTER XL.

SHUT in with closed doors, George Winter
told his tale. Not quite all he could tell;
and not the truth in one very important particular. If that single item of fact might be
kept secret to the end, the speaker's will was
good for it.

They were all standing. Not one sat. And
the room seemed filled with the six men in it,
most of whom were tall. The crimson curtain,
that Annabel Channing had mended, was
drawn before the book-case: on the table-
cover lay pens and ink and paper, for Mr.
Greatorex sometimes wrote at night in his
own room. He and Judge Kene were near
each other; the clergyman was almost within
the shadow of the window-curtain; Bede a
little further behind. On the opposite side
of the table, telling his tale, with the light of
the bright winter's day falling full upon him,

illumining every turn of his face, and, so to say, every word he uttered, was George Winter. And, at right angles with the whole assemblage, his keen eyes and ears taking in every word and look in silence, stood the detective, Jonas Butterby.

Mr. Greatorex, in spite of his son Bede's protestations, had refused to sanction any steps for the release of Alletha Rye from custody. As for Butterby, in that matter he seemed more inexorably hard than a granite stone. " Show us that the young woman is innocent before you talk about it," said they both with reason. And so George Winter was had in to relate what he knew; and Mr. Greatorex—not to speak of some of the rest—felt that his senses were temporarily struck out of him, when he discovered that his efficient and trusted clerk, Brown, was the long-sought after and ill-reputed Godfrey Pitman.

With a brief summary of the circumstances which had led him, disguised, and under the false name of Pitman, to Mrs. Jones's house at Helstonleigh, George Winter passed on to the night of the tragedy, and to the events which had taken him back to the house after his departure from it in the afternoon. If ever Mr. Butterby's silent eyes wore an eager light, it was then : not the faintest turn of a

look, not the smallest syllable was lost upon
him.

"When I had been a week at Mrs. Jones's,
I began to think it might be unsafe to remain
longer," he said; "and I resolved to take my
departure on the Monday. I let it transpire
in the house that I was going to Birmingham
by the five o'clock train. This was to put
people off the scent, for I did not mean to go
by that train at all, but by a later one in an
opposite direction—in fact, by the eight
o'clock train for Oxford: and I had thought
to wait about, near the station, until that
hour. At half-past four I said Good day to
Mrs. Jones, and went out: but I had not gone
many yards from the door, when I saw one of
the Birmingham police, who knew me personally. I had my disguises on, the spec-
tacles and the false hair, but I feared he
might recognize me in spite of them. I
turned my back for some minutes, apparently
looking close into a shop window, and when
the officer had disappeared, stole back to Mrs.
Jones's again. The door was open, and I went
up-stairs without being seen, intending to wait
until dusk."

"A moment, if you please," interrupted Mr.
Greatorex. "It would seem that this was

about the time that Mr. Ollivera returned to Mrs. Jones's. Did you see him?"

" I did not, sir; I saw no one."

" Go on."

" I waited in my room at the top of the house, and when night set in, began to watch for an opportunity of getting away unseen by the household, and so avoid questionings as to what had brought me back. It seemed not too easy of accomplishment : the servant girl was at the street door, and Alfred Jones (as I had learnt his name to be) came in and began to ascend the stairs. When half-way up, he turned back with some gentleman who came out of the drawing-room—whom I know now, but did not then, to be Mr. Bede Greatorex. Alfred Jones saw him to the front door, and then ran up again. I escaped to my room, and locked myself in. He went to his own, and soon I heard him go down and quit the house. In a few minutes I went out of my room again with my blue bag, ready for departure, and stood on the stairs to reconnoitre——"

" Can you explain the cause of those grease spots that we have heard of?" interrupted Bede Greatorex at this juncture. And it might almost have seemed from the fluttering emotion of his tone, which could not be wholly suppressed, that he dreaded the revelation he knew must be coming, and put the question only to delay it.

"Yes, sir. While Alfred Jones was in his room, I dropped my silver pencil-case, and had to light a candle to seek it. I suppose that, in searching, I must have held the candle aside and let the drops of tallow fall on the carpet."

"Go on," again interposed Mr. Greatorex, impatiently. "You went out on the stairs with your bag. What next?"

The witness—if he may be termed such—passed his hand slowly over his forehead before answering. It appeared as though he were recalling the past.

"As I stood there, on the top of the first flight, the sound of voices in what seemed like angry dispute, came from the drawing-room. One in particular was raised in passionate fury; the other was less loud. I did not hear what was said; the door was shut——"

"Were they both men's voices?" interrupted Mr. Ollivera—and it was the first question he had put.

"Yes," came the answer; but it was given in a low tone, and with somewhat of hesitation. "At least, I think so."

"Well."

"The next thing that I heard was the report of a pistol, followed by a cry of pain. Another cry succeeded to it in a different voice, a cry of horror; and then silence supervened."

"And you did not go in?" exclaimed Mr. Ollivera in agitation, taking a step forward.

"No. I am aware it is what I ought to have done; and I have reproached myself later for not having done it; but I felt afraid to disclose to any one that I was yet in the house. It might have led to the discovery of who and what I was. Besides, I thought there was no great harm done; I declare it, upon my honour. I could still hear sounds within the room as of some one, or more, moving about, and I certainly heard one voice speaking low and softly. I thought I saw my opportunity for slipping away, and had crept down nearly to the drawing-room door, when it suddenly opened, very quietly, and a face looked out. Whoever it might be, I suppose the sight of me scared them, for they retreated, and the door was reclosed softly. It scared me also, sending me back up-stairs; and I remained up until the same person (as I supposed) came out again, descended the stairs, and left the house. I got out myself then, gained the railway station by a circuitous route, and got safely away from Helstonleigh."

As the words died upon the ear, there ensued a pause of silence. The clergyman broke it. His mind seemed to be harping on one string.

"Mr. Brown, was that person a man or a woman?"

"Oh, it was a man," answered Mr. Brown, looking down at his waistcoat, and brushing a speck off it with an air of carelessness. But something in his demeanour at that moment struck two people in the room as being peculiar—Judge Kene and Mr. Butterby.

"Should you recognise him again?" continued the clergyman.

"I cannot say. Perhaps I might."

"And you can stand there, Mr. Brown, and deliberately avow that you did not know a murder had been committed?" interposed the sternly condemning voice of Mr. Greatorex.

"On my sacred word of honour, I declare to you, sir, that no suspicion of it at the time occurred to me," answered the clerk, turning his eyes with fearless honesty on Mr. Greatorex. "When I got to learn what had really happened—which was not for some weeks—I wondered at myself. All I could suppose was, that the fear and apprehension I lay under on my own score, had rendered me callous to other impressions."

"Was it *you* who went in, close upon the departing heels of Mr. Bede Greatorex, and did this cruel thing?" asked Judge Kene, with quiet emphasis, as he gazed in the face of the narrator.

"No," as quietly, and certainly as calmly, came the answer, "I had no cause to injure Mr. Ollivera. I never saw him in my life. I am not sure that I knew there was a barrister of the name. I don't think I ever heard of him until after he was in the grave where he is now lying."

"But—you must have known Mr. Ollivera was sojourning in Mrs. Jones's house at the same time that you were?"

"I beg your pardon, Sir Thomas; I did not know that anyone was lodging there except myself. Miss Rye, whom I saw for a few minutes occasionally, never mentioned it, neither did the servant, and they were the only two inmates I conversed with. For all I knew, or thought, Mrs. Jones occupied the drawing-room herself. I once saw her sitting there, and the maid was carrying out the tea-tray. No," emphatically concluded the speaker, "I did not know Mr. Ollivera was in the house ; and if I had known it, I should not have sought to harm him."

The words were simple enough ; and they were true. Judge Kene, skilled in reading tones and looks, saw that much. The party felt at a non-plus : as far as Alletha Rye went, the taking her into custody appeared to have been a mistake.

" You will swear to this testimony of yours, Mr. — Winter ?"

" When you please. The slight amount of facts—the sounds—that reached me in regard to what took place in Mr. Ollivera's room, I have related truthfully. Far from Miss Rye's having had ought to do with it, she was not even in the house at the time : I affirm it as before heaven."

" Who was the man ?" asked Judge Kene— and Mr. Butterby, as he heard the question, gave a kind of derisive sniff. " Come ; tell us that, Mr. Winter."

" I cannot tell you," was George Winter's answer. " Whoever it was, he went down the stairs quickly. I was looking over the top balustrades then, and caught but a transient glimpse of him."

" But you saw his face beforehand ?—when he looked out of the room ?"

" I saw some one's face. Only for a minute.

Had I known what was to come of it later, I might have noticed better."

"And this is *all* you have to tell us?" cried Henry William Ollivera in agitation.

"Indeed it is all. But it is sufficient to exonerate Miss Rye."

"And now, Bede, what do *you* know?" suddenly spoke Mr. Greatorex. "You have acknowledged to me that you suspected at the time it was not a case of suicide."

Bede Greatorex came forward. All eyes were turned upon him. That he was nerving himself to speak, and far more inwardly agitated than appeared on the surface, the two practised observers saw. Judge Kene looked at him critically and curiously: there was something in the case altogether, and in Bede himself, that puzzled him.

"It is not much that I have to tell," began Bede, in answer to his father, as he put his hand heavily on the table, it might be for a support to rest on : and his brow seemed to take a pallid hue, and the silver threads in his once beautiful hair were very conspicuous as he stood. "A circumstance caused me to suspect that it was not a case of suicide. In fact, that it was somewhat as Mr. Brown has described it to be—namely, that some one else caused the death."

A pause of perfect silence. It seemed to Bede that the very coals, cracking in the grate, sounded like thunder.

"What was the circumstance?" asked Mr. Greatorex, for no one else liked to interrupt. "Why did you not speak of it at the time?"

"I could not speak of it then: I cannot speak of it fully now. It was of a nature so —so—so—." Bede came to a full stop: was he getting too agitated to speak, or could he not find a word? "What I would say is," he continued, in a firm low tone, rallying his nerves, "that it was sufficient to show me the facts must have been very much as Mr. Brown now states them."

"Then you only *think* that, Bede?"

"It is more than thinking. By all my hopes of Heaven, I declare that Alletha Rye had not, and could not have had, anything to do with John's death," he added with emotion. "Father, you may believe me: I do know so much."

"But why can you not disclose what it is you know?"

"Because the time has not come for it. William, you are looking at me with re-proachful eyes: if I could tell you more, I would. The secret—so much as I know of it—has lain on me with a leaden weight: I would only have been too glad to disburthen myself of it at first, had it been possible."

"And what rendered it impossible?" questioned the clergyman.

"That which renders it so now. I may not speak; if I might, I should be far more thankful than any of you who hear me."

"Is it a secret of trust reposed in you?"

Bede paused. "Well, yes; in a degree. If I were to speak of what I know, I do not think there is one present"—and Bede's glance ran rapidly over each individual face—"but would hush it within his own breast, as I have done."

"And you have a suspicion of who the traitor was?"

"A suspicion I may have. But for aught else—for elucidation—you and I must be content alike to wait."

"Elucidation!" spoke the clergyman, in something like derision. "It will not, I presume, ever be allowed to come."

"Yes, it will, William," answered Bede, quietly. "Time—events—heaven — all are working rapidly on for it. Alletha Rye is innocent; I could not affirm that truth to you more solemnly if I were dying. She must be set at liberty."

As it was only on the question of her guilt or innocence that the council had been called, it seemed that there was nothing more to do than to break it up. An uncomfortable sensation of doubt, dissatisfaction, and mystery, lay on all. The clergyman stalked away in haughty displeasure. Bede Greatorex, under cover of the crowd, slid his hand gratefully for a moment into that of George Winter, his sad eyes sending forth their thanks. Then he turned to the Judge.

"You can give the necessary authority for the release, Sir Thomas."

"Can I?" was the answer, as Sir Thomas looked at him. "I'll talk about it with Butterby. But I should like to have a private word first with Mr. Winter."

"Why! you do not doubt that she is innocent?"

"Oh dear no; I no longer doubt that. Winter," he added in a whisper, laying his hand on the clerk's shoulder to draw him outside, "*whose face was it that you saw at the door of the room?*"

"Tell him," said Bede suddenly, for he had followed them. "You will keep the secret, Kene, as I have kept it?"

"If it be as I suspect, I *will*," emphatically replied the Judge.

"Tell him," repeated Bede, as he walked away. "Tell him all that you know, Winter, from first to last."

It caused Mr. Greatorex and Butterby to be left alone together. The former, not much more pleased than William Ollivera, utterly puzzled, hurt at the want of confidence displayed by Bede in not trusting him, was in a downright ill-temper.

"What the devil is all this, Butterby?" demanded he. "What does it mean?"

Mr. Butterby, cool as a cucumber, let his eyelashes close for a moment over his non-betraying eyes, and then answered in meek simplicity.

"Ah, that's just it, sir—what it means. Wait, says your son Mr. Bede; wait patiently till things has worked round a bit, till such time as I can speak out. And depend upon it, Mr. Greatorex, he has good cause to give the advice."

"But what can it be that he has to tell? And why should he wait at all to tell it?"

"Well, I suppose he'd like to be more certain of the party," answered Butterby, with a dubious cough. "Take a word of advice from me too, Mr. Greatorex, on this here score, if I may make bold to offer it—*do* wait. Don't force your son to disclose things afore they are ripe. It might be better for all parties."

Mr. Greatorex looked at him. "Who is it that *you* suspect?"

"Me!" exclaimed Butterby. "Me suspect! Why, what with one odd thought or another, I'd as lieve say it must have been the man in the moon, for all the clue we've got. It was not Miss Rye: there can't be two opinions about that. I told you, sir, I had my strong doubts when you ordered her to be apprehended."

"At any rate, you said she confessed to having done it," sharply spoke Mr. Greatorex, vexed with everybody.

"Confound the foolish women! what would the best of 'em not confess to, to screen a sweetheart? Alletha Rye has been thinking Winter guilty all this while, and when it came to close quarters and there seemed a fear that he'd be taken up for it, she said what she did to save him. *I* see it all. I saw it afore Godfrey Pitman was half way through his tale: and matters that have staggered me in Miss Rye, are just as clear to read now as the printing in a big book. When she made that there display at the grave—which you've heard enough of, may be, Mr. Greatorex—she had not had her doubts turned on Godfrey Pitman; she'd thought he was safe away earlier in the afternoon: when she got to learn he had come back again in secret, and was in the house at the time, why then she jumped to the conclusion that he had done the murder. *I* remember."

Mr. Butterby was right. This was exactly how it had been. Alletha Rye had deemed George Winter guilty all along; on his side, he had only supposed she shunned him on account of the affair at Birmingham. There had been mutual misunderstanding; tacit, shrinking avoidance of all explanation; and not a single word of confidence to clear it up. George Winter could not seek to be too explicit so long as the secret he was guarding had to be kept: if not for his own sake, for that of others, he was silent.

"As to what Bede's driving at, and who he suspects, I am in ignorance," resumed Mr. Greatorex. "I am not pleased with his conduct: he ought to let me know what he knows."

"Now, don't you blame him afore you hear his reasons, sir. He's sure to have 'em: and I say let him alone till he can take his own time for disclosing things." Which won't be of one while, was the detective's mental conclusion.

"About Miss Rye? Are you here, Butterby?"

The interruption came from Judge Kene. As he walked in, closing the door after him, they could but be struck with the aspect of his face. It was all over of a grey pallor; very much as though its owner had received some shock of terror.

"What is the matter, Judge?" hastily asked Mr. Greatorex. "Are you ill?"

"I'll? No. Why do you ask? Look so! —Oh, I have been standing in a room without fire and grew rather cold there," carelessly replied the Judge.

CHAPTER XLI.

Lounging quite back in the old elbow horsehair chair, his feet stretched out on the hob on either side the fire, which elegant position he had possibly learnt at Port Natal, sat Mr. Roland Yorke. He had just come home to his five o'clock tea, and took the occasion to indulge in sundry reminiscences while waiting for it to be brought to him. Christmas had passed, these two or three days now; the brief holiday was over, and working days were going on again.

Roland's mood was a subdued one. All things seemed to be, more or less, tinted with gloom. Hamish Channing was dying; a summons had been sent for his friends; the last hour could not now be very far off: and Roland felt it deeply. The ill, worked by his brother Gerald, seemed never to go out of his mind for a moment, sleeping or waking. Vexation of a different kind was also his. Day after day in his sanguine temperament he had looked for a letter from Sir Vincent Yorke, appointing him to the post of bailiff; and no such letter came. Roland, who had heard nothing of the slight accident caused by Gerald (you may be very sure Gerald would not be the one to speak of it), supposed the baronet was in Paris with Miss Trehern. A third source of discomfort lay in the office. Bede Greatorex, whose health since the past few days had signally failed, avowed himself at last unequal to work, and an extra amount of it fell upon his clerks. Roland thought it a sin and a shame that before Christmas Day had well turned, he should have, as he phrased it, to "stick to it like any dray-horse." A rumour had arisen in the office that Bede Greatorex was going away with his wife for change and restoration, and that Mr. Brown was to be head of the department in Bede's place. Roland did not regard the prospect with pleasure : Mr. Brown being a regular martinet in regard to keeping the clerks to their duty.

The grievance that lay uppermost on his mind this evening, was the silence of Sir Vincent. For Hamish he had grieved until it seemed that he could grieve no longer; the rumoured change in the office might never be carried out ; but on the score of Sir Vincent's neglect there was no palliation.

" I'd not treat *him* so," grumbled Roland, his complaint striving to find relief in words. " Even if the place was gone when I applied, or he thought I'd not suit, he might write to me. It's all very fine for him, kicking up his heels in Paris, and dining magnificently in the restaurants off partridges and champagne, and forgetting a fellow as he forgets me ; but if his whole hopes in life lay on the die, he'd remember, I know. If I knew his address over there, I'd drop him another letter and tell him to put me out of suspense. For all the answer that has come to me, one might think he had never had that first letter of mine. He has had it though, and it's a regular shame of him not to acknowledge it, when my heart was set on being able to carry Hamish the cheering news, before he died, that Annabel was provided for. If Dick would only give us a pretty little cottage down yonder and a couple of hundreds a-year ! It wouldn't be much for Dick to give, and I'd serve him bravely day and night. I declare I go into Hamish's room as sheep-faced as a calf, with the shame of having no news to tell. Annabel says—— Oh, it's you, Miss Rye, is it ! Precious cold to-night !"

Miss Rye had come in with the small tea-tray : the servant was busy.   She wore a knot of blue ribbon in her hair, and looked otherwise bright.   Since a private interview held with Mr. Butterby and George Winter, when they returned to release her from custody, she had appeared like a different woman. Her whole aspect was changed : the sad, despairing fear on her face had given place to a look of rest and hope.   Roland had taken occasion to give Mr. Butterby a taste of what that gentleman called " sauce," as to his incurable propensity for apprehending the wrong person, and was advised in return to mind his own business.   While Mrs. Jones had been existing since in a chronic state of tartness ; for she could not come to the bottom of things, and Alletha betrayed anything but a readiness to enlighten her.

" What's for tea ?" asked Roland, lazily, turning his head to get a view of the tray.

" They have boiled you an egg," replied Miss Rye.   " There was nothing else in the house.   Have you seen your letter, Mr. Yorke ?"

" A letter !" exclaimed Roland, starting up with so much alacrity as to throw down the chair, for his hopes suddenly turned to the vainly-expected communication from Sir Vincent. "Where is it? When did it come? Good old Dick!"

It had come just as he went out after dinner, she answered, as she took the letter—which bore a foreign post-mark—from the mantlepiece to hand to him. And eager Roland's spirits went down to zero as he tore it open, for he recognised the writing to be, not Dick Yorke's, but Lord Carrick's.

"Oh, come though, it's rather good," said he, running his eyes down the plain and sprawling hand—very much like his own. "Carrick has come out of his troubles; at least, enough of them to show himself by daylight again in the old country; he will be over in London directly. I say, Miss Rye, I'll bring him here, and introduce him to you and Mrs. J."

And Miss Rye laughed as she left the room more freely than she had laughed for many a day.

"Perhaps Carrick can put me into something!" self-communed Roland, cutting off the top of his egg, and taking in a half-slice of inch-thick bread-and-butter at a bite. "I know he'll not want the will when I tell him about Annabel."

The last morsel was eaten, and Roland was on the point of demanding more, for his appetite never failed, when he heard some one come to the house and enquire for Mr. Yorke. Visions of the arrival of Lord Carrick flashed over him ; he made a dash to the passage, and very nearly threw down a meek little gentleman, who was being shown into his room.

" Halloa !" said Roland, the corners of his mouth dropping with disappointment. " Is it only you ?"

For the visitor was nobody but little Jenner. He had brought a communication from Mr. Greatorex, and took off his hat while he delivered it.

" You are to go back with me to the office at once, if you please, Mr. Yorke. Mr. Greatorex wants you."

" What have I done now ?" questioned Roland, anticipative of a reprimand.

" It is not for anything of that sort, sir. I believe Sir Vincent Yorke has telegraphed for you to go down to him at Sunny Mead. The despatch said you were to lose no time."

Whether Roland leaped highest or shouted loudest, the startled house could not have decided. The anticipated bailiff's place was, in his imagination, as surely his, as though he had been installed in it formally. To wash his hands, brush his hair, and put on a superfine coat took but a minute, before he was striding to the office, little Jenner on the run by his side, and to the presence of Mr. Great-orex.

Into which he went with a burst. The lawyer received him calmly and showed the message from Surrey.

"*Sir Vincent Yorke to Mr. Greatorex.*

"Send Roland Yorke down to me by first train. Lose no time."

"Good old Dick !" repeated Roland, in the fulness of his heart. "I thought he'd remember me ; and there was I, reproaching him like an ungrateful Tom-cat ! It is to appoint me to the bailiff's place, Mr. Great-orex."

"Well—it may be," mused Mr. Greatorex. "But I had fancied the post was filled up."

"Not it, sir. Long live Dick ! When did he come back from Paris ?"

"I know nothing about Sir Vincent's recent movements, Mr. Yorke. You had better be getting to the Waterloo Station. Have you money for the journey ?"

"I've got about sevenpence-halfpenny, sir."

Mr. Greatorex took a half-sovereign from his desk, and ten shillings in silver. "I don't know how often the trains run," he observed, "but if you go at once to the station, you will be all right for the first that starts."

Not to the station, let it start as soon as it would, without first seeing Annabel, and telling her of his good fortune. Away up the stairs went Roland, in search of her, leaping over some boxes that stood packed in the hall; and there he encountered Mr. Bede Greatorex. It was four whole days since Roland had met him, and he thought he had never seen a face so changed in the short space of time. Annabel was not at home, Bede said; she had gone to Mr. Channing's.

"You don't look well, sir."

"Not very, I believe. I am about to try what a month or two's absence will do for me."

"And leave us to old Brown!—that *will* be a nice go!" exclaimed Roland in blank dismay. "But I may not have to stay," he added more brightly, as recollection returned to him. "Vincent Yorke has telegraphed for me, sir, and I and Mr. Greatorex think that he is about to appoint me his bailiff."

A smile crossed the haggard face of Bede. "I wish you success in it," he kindly said.

"Thank you, sir. And I'm sure I wish you and Mrs. Greatorex heaps of pleasure, and

I heartily hope you'll come home strong.   Oh !
and, Mr. Bede—Carrick's coming back."

Bede nodded in answer. Greatorex and
Greatorex knew more of the matter than Roland, since it was they who had intimated to
the peer that the coast was now sufficiently
clear for him.

Roland leaped into a cab, and was taken to
Mr. Channing's. He waited in the empty
dining-room ; and when Annabel came to him,
told her hurriedly of what had happened.
The cab was waiting at the door, Roland was
eager, and her pale cheeks grew rosy with
blushes as he talked and held her hands.

" It can't be for anything else, you know,
Annabel. He is going to instal me off-hand
for certain, or else he would have written and
not telegraphed : perhaps the new bailiff (if
he did appoint one) has turned out to be no
good. There'll be a pretty cottage, I daresay,
its walls all covered with roses and lilies, with
two hundred a year ; and we shall be as happy
as the day's long. You'll not mind trying it,
will you ?"

No, Annabel whispered, the cheeks deep-
ening to crimson, she would not mind trying
it. " I think—I think, Roland," she added,
bending down her pretty face, " that I might

have a pupil if I liked ; and be well paid for
her."

"That's jolly," said Roland. "We might
do, with that, if Dick only offered me one
hundred. He is uncommonly close-fisted.
There'd be a house free, and no end of fruit
and garden-stuff ; and living in the country is
very cheap."

"It is Jane Greatorex."

"Oh *she*," cried Roland, his countenance
falling. "She is a regular little toad, Annabel. I'd not like you to be bothered with
her."

"She would be always good with me. Mr.
and Mrs. Bede are going away, and Mr.
Greatorex does not want us there any longer.
He said a few words to me to-day about my
returning home to mamma at Helstonleigh
and taking Jane with me : that is, if mamma
has no objection. He said he would like Jane
to be with me better than with any one ; and
he'd make it worth my while in point of
salary."

"Then, Annabel, if you don't object to the
young monkey, that's settled, and I shall look
upon it that we are as good as married. What
a turn in fortune's wheel ! Won't I serve
Dick with my best blood and marrow ! I'll
work for him till my arms drop. I say !

couldn't I just see Hamish? I'd like to tell him."

He ran softly up the stairs as he spoke. Hamish was in bed ; and just now alone, save for Miss Nelly, who had rolled herself up on the counterpane like a ball, her cheek close to his. Roland whispered all the items of good news exultantly : it never occurred to him to think that they might turn out to be castles in the air. A smile, partaking somewhat of the old amused character, flitted across Hamish's wasted but still beautiful face and sat in his blue eyes as he listened.

"You'll leave Annabel especially to me, won't you, Hamish ; and wish us both joy and happiness ?"

"I wish you both the best wishes I can wish, Roland—God's blessing," was the low, earnest answer. "His blessing through this life, and in that to come."

Roland bent his face down to Nelly's to hide its emotion, and began kissing her. His grief for Hamish Channing sometimes showed itself like any girl's.

"I have left you her guardian, Roland."

"Me !" exclaimed Roland, the surprise sending him and his wet eyes bolt upright.

"You and Arthur jointly. You will take care of her interests, I know."

"Oh, Hamish, how good of you! Nelly's guardian! *Won't* I take care of her! and love her, too. I'll buy her six-pen'orth of best sugared almonds every day."

Hamish smiled. "Not her personal guardian, Roland; her mother will be that. I meant as to her property."

"Never mind; it's all one. Thank you, Hamish, for your trust in me. Oh, I am proud! And mind that you are a good girl, Miss Nelly, now that I shall have the right to call you to order."

Roland did not seem quite to define the future duties in his own mind. Nelly raised her tear-stained face, and looked at him defiantly.

"I'm going away with papa."

"Not with him, my child," whispered Hamish. "You must stay here a little while. You and mamma will come later."

Nelly burst into sobs. "Heaven is better than this. I want to go there."

"We shall all get there in time, Nelly," observed Roland in much gloom, "but I wish I could have gone now in his stead. Oh, Hamish, I do! I do indeed! Gerald's black work will never be out of my heart. And there's your book getting its crown of laurels at last, and you not living to wear them!"

The gentle face, bright with a light not of this world, was turned to Roland.   " A better crown is waiting for me," he murmured. " My Lord and Master knows how thankfully I shall go to it."

A stamping outside as of an impatient cab-horse on the frosty street, reminded Roland that he was bound on a non-delayable mission. On the stairs he met Annabel, caught hold of her without ceremony, and gave her shrinking face a few farewell kisses.

" Good-bye, darling.   When I come back it will be as bailiff of Sunny Mead."

Roland's delay had been just enough to cause him to miss a train, and the evening was considerably later when he was at length deposited at the small station near Sunny Mead. Looking up the road and down the road in the cold moonlight, uncertain which was his way, he found himself accosted by a man in the garb of a groom.

" I beg pardon, sir : are you Mr. Yorke ?"

" Yes."

" I've got the dog-cart here, sir."

" Oh, have you ?" returned Roland ; " I thought Sunny Mead was close to the station."

" It's a matter of ten minutes' walk, sir ; but they gave me orders to be down, and wait for every train until you came."

"How long has Sir Vincent been back from Paris?" questioned Roland, as they bowled along.

"From Paris, sir? He haven't been to it: not lately. The accident stopped his going."

"What accident?"

Ah! what accident! Roland's eyes opened to their utmost width with surprise, as he listened to the answer.

"Good heavens! And it was caused, you say, by Gerald Yorke?"

"That it was, sir."

"Why, he's my brother."

"Well, sir, accidents happen unintentional to the best of us," observed the man, striving to be polite. "Some of 'em said that the gentleman didn't show himself 'cute at hand-ling of a gun."

"I don't believe he ever handled one in his life before," avowed impulsive Roland. "What a fool he must have been! How is Sir Vincent going on? I'm sure I hope it was no great damage."

"Sir Vincent was going on all right till to-day, sir; and as to the damage, it was not thought to be much. We hear now that it has taken a turn for the worse. They talk of erysipelas."

" Oh, that's nothing," said Roland. " I knew a fellow who got erysipelas in the face at Port Natal till it was as big as a pumpkin, but he did his work all the same. That's it," he mentally decided, as they approached the house. " Poor Dick, confined in-doors, can't look after things himself, and is going to put me to do it."

Upon a flat bed, or couch, in the down-stairs room, where we saw him breakfasting with Gerald, lay Sir Vincent Yorke, his dog beside him. He held out his hand to greet Roland. Impulsively and rather explosively, that unsophisticated African traveller burst out with regrets on the score of the accident, and the more especially that it should have been caused by Gerald.

" Ay, it was a bad job," said Sir Vincent, quietly. " Sit down, Roland. Here, near to me. I am in a good bit of pain, and don't care to talk at a distance."

Roland took the chair pointed to, not a yard off Sir Vincent as he lay, and the two looked at each other. A kind of honest shame was on Roland's face : he was inwardly asking himself how much more disgrace Gerald meant to bring on him. The moderator lamp, a soft, thin perforated paper thrown over to subdue its brightness, was behind the invalid.

"I hope you'll soon be about again, Vincent."

"I hoped so, too, until this morning," was Sir Vincent's answer. "My leg was very uneasy all last night, and I sent at daybreak for the surgeon. He came, and was obliged to tell me that an unfavourable change had taken place: in fact, that dangerous symptoms had set in."

"But you can be cured?" cried Roland.

"No, not now."

"Not be cured!" exclaimed Roland, starting up with wild eyes, and hardly knowing what to understand. "Do you mean, that it will be long first?"

"I mean, that I shall never be cured at all in this world. Sit down, Roland, and listen quietly. The wound, regarded at first as a very simple one, and apparently continuing to progress well, has taken a turn for the worse; and must shortly end in death. Now, do be tranquil, old fellow, and listen. You are my heir, you know, Roland."

Roland, constrained to patience and his chair, stared, and pulled at his whiskers, and stared again.

"Your heir?"

"Certainly. My heir."

The contingency had never, in the whole

course of his life, entered into the imagination of simple Roland. He sat in speechless bewilderment.

"The moment the breath goes out of this poor frail body—and the doctors tell me it will not be many more hours in it now—you will be Sir Roland Yorke. The fourth baronet, and the possessor of the Yorke estates—such as they are."

"Oh, my gracious!" uttered Roland, a vast deal more startled at the prospect than he had been at that of crying hot-pies in Poplar. "Do you mean it, Vincent?"

"*Mean* it! Where are your wits gone, that you need ask? You must know as well as I do that you come next in succession."

"I never thought of it; never once. I don't want it, Vincent, old fellow; I don't, indeed. I hope, with all my heart, you'll get well, and hold it for yourself. Oh, Dick, I hope you will!"

Roland had risen and caught the outstretched hand. As Sir Vincent heard the earnest tones, and saw the face of genuine concern shining out in all its guileless simplicity, the tears in the honest eyes, he came to the conclusion that Roland had been somewhat depreciated among them.

"Nothing can save me, Roland; the doctors have pronounced me to be past human skill, and I feel for myself that I am so. It has not been long, one day, to 'set my house in order,' has it ?"

Amidst Roland's general confusion, nothing had struck him more than the change in Vincent's tone. The old, mincing affectation was utterly gone. A man cannot retain such when brought face to face with death.

" If you could but get well !" repeated poor Roland, rubbing his hot face as he got back to his chair.

" Doctors, lawyers, and parsons—I have had them all here to-day," resumed Sir Vincent. " The first man I sent for, after the fiat was pronounced, was a lawyer from the village hard by : there might not be time, I feared, to get down old Greatorex. He made a short will for me : and it was only when I began to consider what its provisions should be, that I (so to say) remembered you as my heir and successor."

Roland sat, hopelessly listening, unable to take in too much at once.

" The entailed property lapses to you ; but there is some, personal and else, at my own disposal. With the exception of a few legacies, I have bequeathed it all to you, Roland —and you'll be poor enough : and I've appointed you sole executor.   But I think you will make a better man, as the family's head, than I might have made in the long run; and I am truly glad that it is you to succeed, and not Gerald."

Roland gave a groan.

"I allude to his disposition, which I don't think great things of, and to his propensity for spending," continued Sir Vincent. "Gerald would have every acre of the estate mortgaged in a couple of years : I think you will be different.   Don't live beyond your means, Roland ; that's all."

"I'll try to do my very best by everybody," replied Roland.   "As to living beyond my means, Annabel will see to that, and take care of me.   Dick! Dick! it seems so wicked of me to talk coolly of it, as if I were speculating on your death.   I wish you'd try and live!   I don't want the estate and the money; I never thought of such a thing as coming into it.   I rushed down here to-night, hoping you were going to make me your bailiff; and I thought how well I'd try to serve you, and what a good fellow you were for doing it."

"Ah," was the dying man's slight comment, as he drew himself a trifle higher in the bed. "You will be master instead of bailiff; that's all the difference.   I had just engaged a bailiff when you wrote : and I'd advise you to keep him on, Roland, unless you really feel competent to the management yourself."

" I'll keep him on until I've learnt it; that won't be long first. I must have something to employ my time in, Vincent."

" True: I wish I had had it. An idle man must, almost of necessity, glide into various kinds of mischief: of which debt is one."

" You need not fear debt for me, Vincent," was the earnest answer. " I have lived too long on empty pockets, and earned a crust before I eat it, to have ill ways for money or inclination to spend. Why, my best dress suit has been in pawn these two months : and old Greatorex had to advance me twenty shillings to bring me down here."

Something like a smile flitted over Sir Vincent's lips. He pointed to a desk that stood on a side-table.

" When I am gone, Roland, you can open that: there's a little loose cash in it. It will be enough to repay Greatorex and redeem your clothes."

" But I'd not like to take it, Vincent, thank you. I'd not, indeed."

" Why, man ! it will be your own then."

" Oh, well—I never !" cried Roland softly :

quite unable to realize his fast-approaching·
position.

"The danger to some people might lie in
being thus suddenly raised from poverty to
affluence," remarked Sir Vincent. "It has.
shipwrecked many a one."

"Don't fear for me, or for the estate either,.
Vincent. Had this happened some seven or
eight years ago, when I was a lazy, conceited,
ignorant young fool, nearly as stuck-up as
Gerald, I can't say how it might have been.
But I went to Port Natal, you know; and I
gained my life's lesson there. Hamish Channing has left me guardian to Nelly. I can
guess why he did it, too—that the world may
see he thinks me worthy to be trusted at last.
He had always the most delicately generous
heart in Christendom."

"Hamish and I!" murmured Sir Vincent,
in self-communing, "on the wing nearly together."

Yes, it was so. And Roland, with all his
lamentation, could not alter the fiat.

"What was the lesson you learnt at Port
Natal?"

"Not to be a reckless spendthrift; not to
be idle and useless. Vincent," added Roland,
bending his face forward in its strange earnestness, and dropping his voice till it was scarcely

louder than a whisper, "I learnt in Port Natal that there was another world to live for after this: I learnt that our time was not our own to waste in sin, but God's time, given us to use for the best. A chum of mine out there, named Bartle, was struck down by an accident; the doctor said he'd not live the day out—and he didn't. It was a caution to hear his moans and groans, Vincent. He had not been very bad, as far as I knew, in the ways that the world calls bad; he had only been careless and idle, and wasted his days, and never thought of what was to come after. I wish everybody that's the same had seen him die, Vincent, and heard his dreadful cries for mercy. If ever I forget to remember it, I think God would forget me. I saw many such sudden deaths, and plenty of remorse with them, but none as trying as his. It taught me a lesson: brought me to thought, you know. Don't you fear for me, Vincent; it will be all right, I hope: and if I could ever be so foolhardy as to look at a step on the backward route, Annabel would not let me take it."

Roland had spoken in characteristic oblivion that the case, as to the sudden striking down, bore so entire an analogy to the one before him.   Sir Vincent recalled it to him.

"Yes.   Just as it is with me, Roland."

"Oh—but—you've got time yet, you know, Dick," he said, a little confused.   "A parson, who was knocking about, over there, in a threadbare coat, came in and saw Bartle, and talked to him about the thief on the cross. Bartle couldn't see it; his fears didn't let him ; *you* may."

"Yes, yes," replied Sir Vincent, with a half smile, but Roland thought it looked like a peaceful one.   "I have had a parson with me also, Roland."

Roland's face lighted up with a kind of reverence.   Sir Vincent put out his hand and stroked the dog.

"You'll be kind to him, Roland ?"

"Oh, won't I, Dick !   What's his name ?"

"Spot."

"Here !   Spot, Spot !"

"Go, Spot.   Go to your future master."

"Come, then, old fellow.   Spot ! Spot !"

The dog made a sudden leap to the side of Roland at the call, and rubbed his nose against the extended hand.

"I'll be as good to him as if he were a child," spoke Roland, in his earnestness. "See ! we are friends already, Vincent."

And this simple-hearted young fellow was the scapegoat they had all despised! Sir Vincent caught the strong hand and clasped it within his delicate one.

CHAPTER XLII.

A WIDE BLACK BAND ON ROLAND'S HAT.

EARLY in the afternoon and the Waterloo Railway Station. A gentleman got out of a first-class carriage, and made his way to one of the waiting hansoms.

"Stop at the first hatter's you come to," he said to the driver.

Leaping out when his directions were obeyed, he entered the shop, and asked for a mourning band to be put on his hat; a "deep one." You do not need to be told who it was, and what the black band was for. Vincent had died about eight o'clock in the morning, and the Natal traveller was Sir Roland Yorke.

Save for the fact that he had some money in his pockets, in actual reality, which afforded a kind of personal ease to the mind, he was anything but elated at the change of position. On the contrary, he felt very much subdued. Roland could not be selfish, and

the grief and shock brought him by the unexpected death of his cousin Vincent, out-
weighed every thought of self. He had
already tasted some of the fruits of future
power. Servants and others had referred to
him that morning as the new baronet and their
master ; his pleasure had been consulted in
current matters touching the house and estate,
his orders been requested as to the funeral.
Roland was head of all now, the sole master.
Setting aside the sadness that filled his heart
to the exclusion of all else, the very sudden-
ness of the change would prevent him as yet
realizing it in his own mind.

With the conspicuous band on his hat,
stretching up rather above the top of the
crown, Roland entered the cab again, and
ordered it to the office. There he presented
himself to Mr. Greatorex.

"Well ?" said the lawyer, turning round
from his desk. "So you are back again!
What did Sir Vincent want with you ? Has
he made you his bailiff?"

Roland sadly shook his head. And Mr.
Greatorex saw that something was wrong.

"What's amiss ?" he hastily enquired.

"If you please, sir, I am Sir Roland now."

"You are what ?" exclaimed Mr. Greatorex.

"It's only too true," groaned Roland.

"Poor Vincent is dead. Mr. Greatorex, I'd work on all fours for a living to the end of my days if it could bring him to life again. I never thought to come in, I'm sure; and I wouldn't willingly. He died at eight o'clock this morning."

Mr. Greatorex leaned back in his chair and relieved his mind by a pastime he might have caught from Roland—that of staring. Not having heard of Sir Vincent's accident, this assertion of his death sounded only the more surprising. Was Roland telling the truth? He almost questioned it. Roland, perceiving the doubt, gave a summary of particulars, and Mr. Greatorex slowly realized the facts.

Sir Roland Yorke! The light-headed, simple-minded clerk, who had been living on a pound a week and working sufficiently hard to get it, suddenly transformed into a powerful baronet! It was like a romance in a child's fairy tale. Mr. Greatorex rose and held out his hand.

"I must congratulate you on your succession, Sir Roland, sad though the events are that have led to it."

"Now don't! please don't!" interrupted Roland. "I hope nobody will do that, sir: it sounds like a wrong on poor dead Dick. Oh, I'd bring him to life again if I were able."

"I trust you will make us your men of business, Sir Roland," resumed Mr. Greatorex, still standing. "We have been solicitors to the head of the Yorke family in succession for many years now."

"I'm sure if you'll be at the trouble of acting for me, I should like nothing better, sir : bad manners to me if I could have any different thought! And I've put your name and Mr. Bede's down in the list for the funeral, if you'll please attend it. There'll be but a few of us in all. Gerald (though I shouldn't think *he* will show his face at it), William Yorke, Arthur Channing, two or three of Dick's friends, and you and Mr. Bede. Poor Dick said to me when he was dying not to have the same kind of show he had for his father's funeral, he saw the folly of it now, but the quietest I could order. I think he has gone to heaven, Mr. Greatorex."

But that the subject was a solemn one, Mr. Greatorex had certainly laughed at the quaint simplicity of the concluding sentence. One reminiscence in connection with the past funeral rose forcibly in his mind — of the slighting neglect shown to the young man now before him. He, the real heir-presumtive, only that nobody had the wit to think of it, was not deemed good enough to follow his uncle to the grave.   But he stood in his place now.

Bede would not be able to attend the ceremony, Mr. Greatorex said aloud: he was already in France, having crossed over with his wife by the night mail train.

"What is the matter with him?" asked Roland.   "He looked as ill as he could look yesterday."

"I don't know what the matter is," said Mr. Greatorex.   "He has an inward complaint, and I fear it must be making great strides.   His name will be taken out of the firm to-morrow, and give place to Frank's.   It was Bede's own request: it is as if he fears he may never be capable of business again."

"I'm sure I hope he will," cried Roland in his sympathy.   "About me, Mr. Greatorex? Of course I'd not like to leave you at a pinch; I'll come to the office to-morrow morning and do my work as usual for a day or two, until you've found somebody to replace me.   I should like to take this afternoon for myself."

But Mr. Greatorex, with a smile, thought they should not need to trouble Sir Roland: which was no doubt an agreeable intimation: and Roland really had a good deal to do in connection with his new position.

"If I'm not forgetting!" he exclaimed, just

as he was taking his departure. "There's the money you lent me, sir, and I thank you for the loan of it."

In taking the sovereign from his pocket, he pulled out several. Mr. Greatorex jokingly remarked that he had apparently no longer need to borrow.

"It is from poor Dick's desk," sadly observed Roland. "He told me there was enough money in it to repay the pound to you and get my clothes out of pawn, and that it would be all my own when he died. Well, what do you think I found there when I opened it to-day?—Nearly a hundred pounds in gold and bank notes!"

"But you have not got all that about you, I hope?"

"Yes I have, sir; it was safer to bring it up than to leave it. I shall pay it into the banker's. I've got to show myself there, I suppose, and leave my signature in their books; it won't be so neat a one as poor Dick's."

Roland departed. Looking in for a moment at the office as he went out, and announcing himself as Sir Roland Yorke, upon which Mr. Hurst burst out laughing in his face. He dashed in on Mrs. Jones with his news, eat nearly the whole of a shilling Madeira cake that happened to be on the table, while he talked, and made a voluntary promise to that tart and disbelieving matron to refurnish her house from top to bottom. Then the cab was ordered to the bankers', where his business was satisfactorily adjusted. Gerald's chambers were not far off, and Roland took them next. The servant met him with the bold assertion that his master was out.

"Don't bother yourself to deny him, my good man ; I saw his face at the window," said Roland, with frankness. "You may safely show me in : I am not a creditor."

"Well, sir, we are obliged to be excessively cautious, just now, and that's the truth," apologised the man in a tone of confidence. "Mr. Yorke, I think ?"

"Sir Roland Yorke," corrected Roland.

"*Sir?*" returned the man, looking at him as if he thought he saw a lunatic.

"Sir Roland Yorke," was the emphatic repetition. "Have the goodness to announce me."

And the servant opened the room door and did it.

As Roland saw Gerald's quick look of surprise, he would, under other circumstances, have shaken in his shoes at the fun. But sadness wholly reigned over him to-day. And

—if truth must be told—a terrible aversion to Gerald for his work and its fruits held possession of the new heir.

"Oh it's you," cried Gerald, roughly. "What on earth possessed the fellow?"

"The fellow did right, Gerald. I gave him my name, and he announced it."

"Don't come here with your fool's blabber. He said 'Sir Roland Yorke.'"

"And it is what I am."

Gerald's face grew dark with passion. He had an especial dislike to be played with.

"Vincent's dead, Gerald."

"It is a lie."

"Vincent died this morning at eight o'clock," repeated Roland. "I was with him: he telegraphed for me yesterday. Look at this mourning band"—showing his hat—"I've just been to get it put on. Do you think I'd have the face to invent a jest on this subject? Vincent Yorke is dead, poor fellow, and I have come into things as Sir Roland. Not that I can fully believe it myself yet."

The tone of the voice, the deep black band, and a kind of subtle instinct within himself brought conviction of the truth home to Gerald Yorke. Had it been to save his fame, he could not have helped the loud brazen tone from going out of his voice, or the dread that took possession of his whole aspect.

"What—has—he—died—of?"

"The gunshot wound."

A pause. Gerald broke it.

"It was going on well. I heard so only two days ago."

"But it took a sudden turn for the worse; and he is dead."

Gerald's face assumed a tinge as of bluish chalk. Was he to have *two* lives on his soul? Hamish Channing's had surely been enough for him without Vincent Yorke's. Pushing back his damp hair, he met Roland's steady look, and so made believe to feel nothing, went to the fire, and stirred it gently.

"Why did the doctors let it take *this* turn?" he asked, flinging down the poker. "It was as simple a wound as ever was given."

"I suppose they'd have helped it, if they could."

Another pause.

"Well—of course—as you *have* succeeded, I must congratulate you," said Gerald stiffly and lamely. Absently, too, for he was buried in thought, reflecting on what an idiotic policy his, to Roland, had been : but this contingency had never occurred to him more than it had to Roland.

"Vincent had a good lot of property that was not entailed," resumed Gerald. "Do you know who he has willed it to? Did he make a will?"

"He made a will yesterday, before telegraphing for me."

Gerald lifted his face with a transient hope.

"I wonder if he has remembered me?"

"I think not. Except some legacies to the servants, and a keepsake for Miss Trehern— his watch and diamond ring, I fancy—he said nobody's name was mentioned in the will but mine. It has not been opened: I thought I'd leave it till after the funeral. I am the executor."

"*You!*—you don't want his ready money as well as his inheritance," spoke Gerald, in a foam.

"I'm sure I didn't want any of it, I only thought to be his bailiff; but I can't help it if it has come to me," was Roland's quiet answer, as he turned to depart. "Good afternoon, Gerald. I thought it right to call and tell you of his death: you may like to draw your blinds down."

"Thanks," said Gerald, sarcastically.

"You will receive an invitation to the

funeral, Gerald. But I'd like to intimate that if you do not care to attend, I shall not look upon it in the light of a slight," added candid Roland, who really spoke in simple good nature. "We shall be enough without you if you'd rather stay away."

Before Gerald's awful rage at the speech was over, for he looked upon it as bestowed in a patronising light from the new baronet, Roland was vaulting into the waiting cab. Gerald had the pleasure of peeping on from the window.

"Sir Roland Yorke!—Sir Roland Yorke!" he spoke aloud in his horrible mortification. "Sunny Mead for his home, and four thousand a year landed property, and heaps of ready money. Curse the beggar! Curse the shot that has brought him the luck of the inheritance! I'd sell my soul for it to have been mine. I should wear the honours better than he. I wish to heaven he could die to-night!"

And Mr. Gerald Yorke, looking after the receding cab with a dark and sullen countenance, could indeed have sold his soul; if by so doing he might have annihilated his brother and stepped into his place. He was in that precise frame of mind for which some few men in the world's actual history, and a vast many in fiction, have stained their hands with crime for the greed of gain.

✳　　　✳　　　✳　　　✳　　　✳

Tread lightly, speak softly; for death is already hovering in the chamber. As Roland enters on tiptoe he takes in the scene at a glance. Hamish lying with closed eyes, and the live ball, Miss Nelly, tucked outside beside him, her golden curls mingling with his damp hair. A sea of old Helstonleigh faces seems to be gathered round; save that Roland silently clasps Arthur's hand, he takes notice of none. Edging himself between Annabel and Tom Channing, as they stand side by side, he bends his face of concern downwards. The slight stir arouses Hamish, he opens his eyes, and holds up his feeble hand with a remnant of the old smile.

"Back again! Head bailiff?"

Roland bit his lip. His chest was heaving with emotion, his face working. Hamish, who retained his keenest perceptive faculties to the last, spoke again in his faint voice.

"Is it good news?"

"It's good news. Good news, Hamish, and at the same time awfully bad. Vincent's dead, and I'm—I'm in his shoes."

Hamish did not seem to understand. Neither did the others.

"It's me to come after him, poor fellow, you see.   I am Sir Roland now."

As the words fell upon the previously silent room, you might have heard a pin drop. Cheeks flushed, eyes looked out their questioning surprise at the speaker.   Upon Hamish alone the communication seemed to make no impression : earthly interests were to him now as nothing.

"You will give me Annabel with a will, Hamish, now that I have come into the family inheritance ?"

"I had already given her to you, so far as my best will was good to do it.   Roland—"

The voice seemed to be fading away altogether, but in the eyes there was an eager gaze.   Roland bent his head lower to catch the sounds about to issue from the lips.

"There's a different and a better inheritance, Roland ; one of love, and light, and everlasting peace.   You will both of you strive for that."

"Yes, that we will.   And gain it too.   Oh, Hamish, if you could but stop with us a bit longer!" burst forth Roland, letting his suppressed emotion come out with a choking sob. "It's nothing all round but dying.   First

Vincent, and now you! I never knew such a miserable world as this. I'd have laid down my own life to keep either of you in it."

There stole a smile of ineffable peace over the dying face. It seemed to have caught a ray of the heavenly light in which it would so soon be shining.

CHAPTER XLIII.

IT is certainly not often in this life that improbable dreams of fame and fortune get to be realized as they were in the case of Roland Yorke. Down he went to his native place, Helstonleigh, in all the glory of fame and fortune that his imagination had been wont to picture; the dog, Spot, with him. He paid his creditors their debts twice over; he made presents to his mother and the world; he went knocking at old Galloway's door, and caused himself to be fully announced, as he had at Gerald's—Sir Roland Yorke. He ran in and out of the proctor's office at will, took possession of his former stool there, and answered callers as if he were the veritable clerk he used to be. He promised a living to Tom Channing, promotion in India to Charley; made a sweeping bow to William Yorke the first time he met him in the street, and called out to know whether he might be considered

a scape-goat still. He put up a tombstone to
commemorate the virtues of Jenkins. Meeting Harry Huntley, he nearly cried over
Hamish. Hamish Channing's book was at
length in every heart and home—ah, that he
had lived to see it! The good had all come
too late for *him*. Ellen would be wealthy
from henceforth, for her father had regained
his fortune ; her aunt, stiff Miss Huntley, had
died, and bequeathed to her the whole of
hers ; and little Miss Nelly was an heiress.

Not immediately, however, had Roland
hastened to quit London for Helstonleigh,
and there's something to tell about it. He
had affairs to attend to first ; and it took him
some time to forget his daily sorrow for the
dead. Roland's private belief was that he
should never cease to mourn for Hamish ;
should never rise in the morning, or go to rest
at night, without thinking of him and Gerald's
miserable work. He entered on his abode at
Sunny Mead, his home from henceforth, made
himself acquainted with his future position,
and what his exact revenues would be. In
his imperfect way, but honest wish to do
right, he apportioned out plenty of work for
himself, and not much to spend, resolving
above all things to eschew a life of frivolity
and idleness. Roland would rather have fol-

lowed the plough's tail day by day, than sink to that.

The first few weeks he divided his time between Sunny Mead and London. When in town, he dropped in upon his old friends with native familiarity: prosperity and a title could not change Roland. The office and clerks saw him very often; Mrs. Jones's tea and muffins occasionally suffered by a guest who had a large appetite. He re-furnished that tart lady's house for her after a rather sharp battle; for at first Mrs. J. would not accept the boon. The first visitor Roland had the honour of entertaining was Lord Carrick. His white-haired lordship was flourishing in London again, and gave Roland a whole week of his hearty, genial, good-natured company at Sunny Mead.

The thorn in the flesh was Gerald, and it happened that Mr. Gerald's career came to a crisis during the week of Lord Carrick's stay at Sunny Mead. On the last day of it, when they were out in the frost, and the peer was imparting to his nephew sundry theories for the best cultivation of land, a servant ran out to announce the arrival of a lady, who had come in great haste from the railway station. She appeared to be in distress, the man added, and said she must at once see Sir Roland.

In distress beyond doubt : for when Roland went clattering in, wondering who it could be, there met him the tear-stained face of Winny. She had brought down a piteous tale. Gerald, arrested the previous day, had lodgings in that savoury prison, Whitecross Street; he had boldly sent her to ask Roland to pay his debts and set him free. Winny, sobbing over some luncheon that Roland good-naturedly set her down to at once, protested that she felt sure one at least of the three little girls would be found in the fire when she got back to them.

Lord Carrick drew Roland aside.

" I'm not ill-natured, me boy, as ye knew long ago, and I'd do a good turn for anybody ; but I'd like to give ye a caution. *Don't begin by paying Gerald's debts.* If ye do, as sure as ye're a living man, ye'll never have a minute's peace for him to the last day of ye're life. Set him free now, and all his thanks would be to run up more for ye to pay. In a year's time he'd be in the same plight again ; and he or his creditors would be bothering ye always. *Don't begin it.* Let him fight out his debts as he best can."

" It's just what I'd like to do," said Roland. " I'd not mind allowing a couple of hundred a year, or so, for Winny and the children. I meant to offer it. It might be paid to her

weekly, you know, uncle, and I could slip
something more into her hand whenever we
met. She might get a bit of peace then. But
I don't think it would be doing Gerald any
real kindness in the long run to release him
from his debts."

Lord Carrick nodded most emphatically.

"I need not tell Winny this, Uncle Carrick—only that she and the kittens shall be
taken care of from henceforth. She can carry
a sealed note back to Gerald."

"*I'll* see to him," said Lord Carrick. "If
he is to get any help at all, it must be from
me. Ye can write the note to him. It would
be the worst day's work ye ever entered on if
ye attempted to help him. It is nothing else
but helping people, Roland, me boy, that has
kept me down, and I'd not like to see you
begin it. If Gerald can't get clear without
assistance, I may come to the rescue later.
But he'll have to try."

"Perhaps I might be got to allow him a
hundred a year, or so, for himself later," added
relenting Roland. "But I'll never have anything to do with his debts, or suffer him to
look to me to pay them."

Could Gerald, in his distant and gloomy
abode, but have heard this, he had surely
been ready to shoot the pair of speakers; and

with more intentional malignity, too, than he had shot Sir Vincent.

But we began the chapter at Helstonleigh. For once in its monotonous life that faithful city had found something to arouse it from its jog-trot course ; and people flew to their doors and windows to gaze after Sir Roland Yorke. It did not seem much less improbable that the time-honoured cathedral might some night disappear altogether, than that the once improvident school-boy of not too good repute, the careless run-a-gate who had made a moonlight flitting, and left some fifty pounds' worth of debts behind him, should come back Sir Roland, like a hero of romance.

Fruition never answers to anticipation—as Roland found, now that his golden visions came to be realised. The romantic charm of the oft-pictured dream was wanting ; the green freshness of sanguine boyhood no longer threw its halo on his heart ; the vivid glow of imaginative hope had mellowed down to a sober tint. In manner, in gleeful frankness, Roland was nearly as impulsive and boyish as ever ; but his mind had gained a good deal of experience, and reflection had come to him. The chances and changes of the world had worked their effect ; and the deaths, caused directly or indirectly by Gerald, sat heavily on his generous heart. Adam's curse lies on all things, and there can be no pleasure without pain.

Roland did not miss it. Enough of charm was left to him. Annabel was staying with her mother, and things seemed to have gone back again to the dear old days before Roland had known the world, or tasted of its cares. Roland went calling upon his acquaintance continually, distant and near, making himself at home everywhere. Ellen Channing, worn to a thread-paper with grief, was visiting her father in her maiden home. Nelly made its charm now. The young widow would probably take up her abode at Helstonleigh, in spite of Roland's strong advice that it should be near Sunny Mead.

"I told you I should be sure to get on and make my fortune sometime, Mr. Galloway."

The old proctor, whose health was failing hopelessly, returned a slighting answer. Roland, without ceremony as usual, had dashed into the office, and was sitting on a high desk with his legs dangling. The remark was given in return for some disparaging observation as to Roland's former doings.

"*You* made it! Ugh! A great deal of that."

"Oh—well—I've come into one, at any rate."

"The only way you were ever likely to attain to one. Left to your own exertions, you'd have got back here with holes in your breeches."

"Now don't you be personal, sir," was the laughing rejoinder. "I'm Sir Roland Yorke, you know."

"And a fine Sir Roland you'll be!"

"I'll try and be a good one," said Roland emphatically, as he caught Arthur's eye—who was seated in the place of state as the head of the office, for the proctor had virtually resigned it. "Arthur knows he can trust me now : ask him, else, sir. Hamish knew it also before he died."

"I should like to hear what business he had to die, and who killed him?" cried old Galloway explosively. "It was done amongst you, I know. A nice thing for my old friend Mr. Huntley to get back to England and find his son-in-law dead : the bright, true young fellow that he loved as the apple of his eye."

"Yes, I think he was killed among us, up there," sadly avowed Roland, his honest face kindling with shame. "But I did not help in it, Mr. Galloway ; I'd have given my life to save his. I wish I could!"

"Wishes won't bring him back. I saw his wife yesterday—his widow, that is. I'm sure I couldn't bear to look at her."

"Did you see sweet little Nelly?" cried Roland eagerly, his thoughts taking a turn. "If ever I have a girl of my own, I hope she'll be like that child."

"Now just you please to take yourself off, Sir Roland, and come in when we're a little less busy," returned the proctor, who was very much out of sorts that morning. "You are hindering business, just as you used to."

But perhaps the greatest of all small delights was that of encountering Mr. Butterby. Roland had just emerged from the market house one Saturday, where he had been in the thick of the throng, making himself at home, and enquiring affably the price of butter of all the faces he remembered, and been seduced into buying a tough old gander, on the grave assurance that it was a young and tender goose, when he and the detective met face to face.

"Well?" said Roland, dangling the goose in his hand, as unblushingly as though it had been a bouquet of choice flowers.

"Well?" returned Mr. Butterby. "How are you, sir? I heard you were down here."

"Ay. I've come to set things straight that I left crooked. And glad to be able to do it at last.   You've heard about me, I suppose, Butterby?"

"*I*'ve heard," assented Butterby. "You are Sir Roland Yorke, and have come into the family estates and honours, through the untimely death of Sir Vincent. A lucky shot for you, sir."

"Lucky?" groaned Roland.   "Well, in one sense I suppose it was : but don't go and think me a heartless camel, Butterby.   I declare to you that if I could bring Sir Vincent back, though I had to return to my work again, and the turn-up bedstead at Mrs. J.'s, I'd do it this minute cheerfully.   When I sat by, watching him die, knowing he was going to make room for me, I felt downright wicked : almost as bad as my nice brother must have felt, who shot him.   Did you read about it in the newspapers ?—they had got it all as pat as might be.   I can't think, for my part, how they lay hold of things."

Butterby nodded assent.   There was little he did not read, if it could in the remotest degree concern him.

"I'm paying up, Butterby.   Paying everybody, and something over.   If ever I get into debt again call me an owl.   Galloway groans and grunts, and says I shall; but I fancy he knows better.   What do you think ?

He took his hat off to me in the street yesterday! formerly he'd hardly nod to me over his shoulder sideways."

"How were the folks up yonder, Sir Roland, when you left?" asked Butterby, jerking his head in the direction of London. "Is Miss Rye all right?"

"Oh, she's uncommon jolly. The last day I called there, Mrs. J. said she supposed she and Winter—they call him Winter now—would be making a match of it. Upon that, I told Miss Rye I'd buy her the wedding dress. Instead of being properly grateful, she advised me not to talk so fast. I say, Butterby, that *was* a mistake of yours, that was—the taking her into custody for the one that killed John Ollivera."

"Ay," carelessly returned Mr. Butterby, with a kind sniff. "The best of us go in for mistakes, you know."

"I suppose *you* can't help it, just as some people can't help dreaming," observed Roland with native politeness. "I went up and saw his grave yesterday. I say, shall you ever pitch upon the right one?"

But that Mr. Butterby turned his eyes away towards the Guildhall opposite before he answered, Roland might have observed a peculiar shade cross their steady light. Whatever curious outlets his speculations had drifted to in the course of years, as to the slayer of Mr. Ollivera, he knew the truth now.

"Shan't try at it, sir. Take it from first to last, it has been about the queerest case that ever fell under mortal skill; and we are content for the future to let it be."

"I won't forget you, Butterby. You've not been a bad one on the whole. A snuff-box would be of no use, you said; but you shall have something else. And look here, if ever you should come within range of my place in Surrey, I'd be glad to see you there for half an hour's chat. Good-day, old Butterby. Isn't this a prime goose? I've just been giving seven shillings for it."

He and his ancient goose went vaulting off. Roland frequently took articles home to help garnish Lady Augusta's dinner-table; very much to the wrath of the cook, who found she had double work.

But it must not be thought Roland led entirely an idle life at Helstonleigh. Apart from personal calls on his friendship, in the shape of dropping in upon people, he had work on his hands. By Mrs. J.'s permission he was replacing the plain stone on poor Jenkins's grave with one of costly marble.

Roland himself undertook the inscription. Not being accustomed to composition, he found it a puzzling task.

" Here's to the memory of JOSEPH JENKINS. He was too good for this world, inoffensive as a young sparrow, and did everybody's work as well as his own. Put upon by the office and people in general, he bore it all meekly, according to his nature, never turning again. A cough took him off to Heaven, leaving Mrs. J. behind, and one or two to regret him, who knew his virtues. This tribute is erected by his attached friend, (who was one of the worst to put upon him in life,) and sorrowful, ROLAND YORKE."

Such was the inscription for the marble tomb-stone, as it went in to the sculptor. That functionary suggested some slight alterations, which Sir Roland was reluctant to accede to. There ensued writing and counter writing, and the epitaph, finally inscribed, contained but little (like some bills that pass through Parliament) of the original.

And so the sweet days of spring glided on, and the time came for Roland to depart. To depart until June, when he would return to claim his bride. Tom Channing should

marry them, and nobody else, avowed Roland;
and if the Reverend Bill put up his back at
not having the first finger in the pie, why he
must put it up. Annabel was his confident
in all things; and Annabel thought she
should rather be married by her brother, than
by William Yorke.

The once happy home of the Channings
bore the marks of time's chances and changes.
The house was the same, as were its elements
for peace, but some of its inmates had quitted
it for ever. Mrs. Channing, Arthur, Tom,
Charles, and Annabel : they moved about in
their mourning garments, with their regretful
faces, thinking ever of him who had whilom
made its sunshine, Hamish the bright. He
had gone to a better world, where there was
neither pain nor tears, neither cruel injustice
nor heart-breaking sorrow; but this consola-
tion is always hard to realize, and their grief
was lasting. Mrs. Channing looked aged and
worn; the boys and girls had grown into
men and women; in old Judith and her
snow-white mob-cap, there alone appeared to
be no change.

It was at length the day of Roland's departure, and he was holding a final interview
with Annabel. They stood at the glass doors
of the study window, open to the garden,

and the warm May sun shone in gaily, making the crape on Annabel's silk dress look hot and rusty. The once untidy study, when they were all boys and girls together, had been renovated with a green carpet and delicately-papered walls ; the young parson now called it his.

Considering Roland's deficiencies on the score of forethought, he had really organized the plans for his future life with a great deal of wisdom. Sunny Mead was to be their sole home, and Annabel chief cash-keeper in regard to ready money. On that he was resolved, honestly avowing that he was not to be trusted with money in his pocket : it was sure to *go*. The residence in Portland Place, which Sir Richard had only held on a lease, had been given up : there was to be no town house, no fashion, no gaiety. Annabel seconded him in all, urging moderation strenuously. He was going up now to make his bow to the Prince of Wales at a levée : and it was to be hoped he would accomplish it with passable decorum : and Annabel would be presented to the Queen on the first favourable opportunity, after she should be Lady Yorke. So far, that was due from their position ; but there the exigencies of fashionable society would for them end. Sunny Mead would be their home ; and, it could not be doubted, a very happy one. They are talking of the prospect, now as they stand together : and to both it is one of rose colour.

"But for going to Port Natal, Annabel, there's no knowing how I might have turned out —a regular drawling idler about town, as some of the Yorkes have been before me. I might have gone in for all kinds of folly, and come to no end of grief. We shall be safe down at Sunny Mead, and live like—like—" Roland stops for a simile.

"Rational people," puts in Annabel with a smile.

"Fighting-cocks," says Roland. "I shall make a good farmer."

"But, Roland," she rejoins, dubiously, "I hope you'll not discharge the bailiff until you feel that you are fully competent to the management. You don't know much of farming yet."

"Not know much of farming !" exclaims Roland, his eyes opening with surprise. "After all my experience at Port Natal ! Look at the pigs I had to manage—obstinate, grunting animals—and the waggons and carts I was put to drive—filled with calves some-times ! I'm not obliged to take the threshing and mowing myself, you know. As to the bailiff, he shall stay on until you send him away, if it's two years to come."

She bends her blushing face a little forward, plucking an early rose-bud. Roland takes it from her and puts it in his coat. On her finger flashes a valuable diamond ring, the pledge of their engagement.

"We won't have a frying-pan in the house, Annabel. I can't bear to see one since that failure at Port Natal."

She turns her laughing eyes on him. Roland honestly thinks they are the truest, sweetest, best the world ever contained, and feels he can never be thankful enough that he is to call them his.

CHAPTER XLIV.

THE summer and the day were alike on the wane. It was the end of July, and a dull evening. Mr. Greatorex was sitting alone in the coming twilight, in the large and handsome dining-room, where we first saw him at the beginning of this history. Haggard he had looked then, waiting to hear the particulars of his favourite nephew's death; far more haggard he looked now, for the truth in regard to it was at length disclosed to him.

He wore deep mourning. The son, whose appearance of ill health had of late given him so much concern, was dead: Bede. Alas! it was not illness of body that had ailed Bede Greatorex, and turned his days to one ever-moving, never-ceasing tumultuous sea of misery, but that far worse affliction, illness of mind. In bodily sickness there may arise intervals of light, when the suffering is not felt so keenly, or the heavenly help is nearer for support; in mental sickness, grave as Bede's was, such intervals never come.

After quitting home at the turn of Christmas, and travelling for a month or two hither and thither, Bede settled down in a remote French town. There was a very small colony of English in it, and an English chaplain, who did the duty for nothing. Bede had not intended to make it a permanent halting place, but his weakness increased greatly, and he seemed never willing to attempt another move onwards. Mrs. Bede grumbled woefully: she called the town a desert and their lodgings a barn: truth to say, the rooms were spacious and had as good as nothing in them. She amused herself—such amusement as it was—by taking drives in the early spring freshness, and talking French, for improvement, with a fashionable Parisian femme de chambre, whom she had found herself lucky enough to engage. In June Bede died: and the date of his death happened, by a rather singular coincidence, to be that of Roland Yorke's wedding day. But that can pass.

With Bede's death, a month ago now, things in the office had undergone some fresh arrangements. Frank Greatorex was his father's sole partner in the practice. Frank was soon to bring home his wife: and it was

to be hoped she would make a happier home
of the dwelling than its late mistress had
done.   There could be little doubt of it : and
Mr. Greatorex stood a fair chance of regaining
some of his domestic comfort.   The prospects
of Bede's widow were not flourishing.   Bede
had not left a shilling behind him ; a little
debt, in fact, instead; that is, *she* was in debt:
and the bills for his funeral and other in-
cidental expences, had come over to Mr.
Greatorex.   There had been no marriage set-
tlement on Louisa Joliffe : she was now left
to the mercy of her father-in-law: and though
a generous man by nature and habit, Mr.
Greatorex was not showing himself generous
in this.   In a cool, business-like letter, conveyed to her personally by a trust-worthy
clerk, Mr. Greatorex had informed her that
henceforward she would be allowed two hundred pounds a year.   One hundred pounds in
addition he made her a present gift of.   The
clerk, despatched with the letter and money,
was Mr. Brown, who had entirely resumed
his name of Winter : the office, not getting
into the new habit readily, usually called him
Mr. Brown-Winter.   Mr. Winter was commis-
sioned to discharge the above-mentioned bills,
and to see a stone placed over the grave, the
inscription for which had been written down

by Mr. Greatorex. It was short as might be :
only the following words, with the date of
death.

BEDE GREATOREX.

AGED THIRTY-NINE.

" Come unto me all ye that labour and are heavy laden."

Mr. Winter had executed his charges, and
was back again. The clerks heard with very
little surprise that he was to be promoted
amidst them : the confidential manager in
future under Mr. Greatorex and his son ; one
to whom the office would have to look up to
as a master. Rumour went that Mr. Winter
was about to become a qualified solicitor : not
from any view of setting up for himself, but
that he might be more efficient for his duties
in the house of Greatorex and Greatorex.
His salary would be handsome : it had been
already considerably augmented since the
month of January last. Mr. Winter had
taken a small, pretty house, and would soon
bring a wife home to it : Alletha Rye was to
exchange her name to Alletha Winter. The
clerks in general looked upon it that Mr.
Winter's promotion took its rise in his un-
doubted business merit and capacity : but in
point of fact it was owing to a few lines

written by Bede to his father. "The man is of sterling merit : he has forgotten self in striving patiently to benefit and shield me : reward him for my sake. I am sure he will repay in faithfulness all you can do for him."

Little more than this did Bede say ; not a word as to the nature of what the benefit or the shielding had been. Mr. Greatorex knew now, for a revelation had been made to him through Judge Kene. Bede, only the day before his death, had posted a letter to Sir Thomas Kene, one that he had spent a week in writing, getting to it at intervals.

The anguish that communication, and other things, brought to Mr. Greatorex, was very sharp still. He was feeling it as he sat there in the evening twilight. Bede's death he had, in one sense, almost ceased to mourn : knowing now what a happy release from mental pain it must have been. But he could not think with the smallest patience of Bede's wife : never again, never again. *She* had been the primary author of all the misery : but for her, his son—ay, and some one else, dear to him as a son—had been, in all human probability, living now, happy, peaceful, and playing a good and busy part on the world's stage.

"Will you admit visitors, sir ?"

"Eh ! what !"—and Mr. Greatorex started

up half in alarm as the servant spoke, so deeply had he been buried in far-away thoughts. "Visitors this evening!—no. Stay, Philip. Who are they?"

"Sir Roland and Lady Yorke, sir."

"Oh, I'll see them," said Mr. Greatorex. "Ask them to walk up."

Roland and his wife, passing through London from their wedding tour, part of which had been spent in Ireland, at Lord Carrick's, had halted for a night at one of the hotels. "To see old friends," said Roland. Not that he had many to see : Mrs. J. and Mr. Greatorex nearly comprised them. Winny Yorke and her children were in Wales with her mother. Gerald had sent them, "as a temporary thing," till he could get "a bit straight." When that desirable epoch might be expected to dawn, was hidden in the mystery of the future. Gerald had been a good month in Whitecross Street prison, done to death pretty nearly with his creditors' reproaches, who used to go down in a body to abuse him, when they found there was no chance of their getting a farthing. He and his chambers had been sold up ; and altogether Gerald had come to considerable grief. Just now he was in Paris, enjoying himself on a sum of money that Lord Carrick had been

induced to give him, and on the proceeds from
an article that he supplied twice a week to a
London newspaper.   He thought himself ter-
ribly hard worked ; and slightly relieved his
bile by telling everybody that his brother
Roland was the greatest villain under the sun.
Roland meant to find him a post if he could,
and meanwhile took care of Winny and the
little ones : Gerald quietly ignored that.

"Sir Roland and Lady Yorke."

Mr. Greatorex met them with outstretched
hands, giving Annabel a fatherly kiss on her
blushing face.   He quite forgot her new
elevation, remembering her only as the sweet
and simple girl who had made sunshine in his
house at odd moments. She looked sweet
and simple, still quite unaltered. Roland, on
his part, had not attained the smallest additional dignity : he clattered in just as of
yore.   They were going to Sunny Mead on
the morrow, and he began telling of his future
plans for the happy home life.

Mr. Greatorex smiled as he listened. "I
don't fancy you will give us much work,
Sir Roland, in the way of incurring debts and
trouble, and coming to us to get you clear of
them," he observed.

"No thank you, I leave that to Gerald.
Mr. Greatorex," added Roland, his eyes

shining with honest light, his face meeting
that of his ex-master, " I promised Vincent
when he was dying that I'd keep clear of
trouble ; I as good as promised Hamish : I'd
not go from my word to *them*, you know.
And, what's more, I shall never wish to."

" I see. You will be a dead loss to us.
The Yorkes in general have been profitable
clients."

Roland took the words seriously, and his
mouth fell a little.

" I'm very sorry, sir. I—I'll give you a present every year to make up for the deficiency,
if you'll accept it. A golden inkstand, or
something of that sort."

Mr. Greatorex looked at him with a smile,
never speaking. Roland resumed, thoroughly
in earnest, his voice low.

" It's such an awful deal of money, you see ;
four thousand a year, besides a house and lots
of other things. Two people could never
spend it, and if we could, we don't think it
would be doing right. Annabel and I see
things alike. We mean to put aside half of
our income ; against a rainy day, say ; or—
there are so many people who want help. You
see, Mr. Greatorex, we had both learnt to
live on little. But I'm sure I shall be sorry,
if you look upon me as a loss."

"You can repay me, Roland, better than by a golden inkstand," said Mr. Greatorex, laying his hand on the young man's shoulder. "Let me come to you for a week annually when the summer roses are in bloom; and do you tell me, year by year, that you have adhered to your proposed simple mode of life."

Roland was in the skies at once. "It is a bargain, mind that," he said. "You will come to us always with the summer roses. As to a week only, we'll talk about that."

"And Jane shall meet you, sir," interposed Annabel with shy joy. "She is very happy at her school; I often have letters from her. Roland and I were thinking of having her at Christmas, if you don't mind."

"And Nelly Channing too, if her mother will spare her," put in Roland. "And we have talked about those three little mites in Wales. It would be good to have the lot together, and give them a bit of pleasure. They should have a jolly Christmas tree; and we'd get over some boxes of Lumps of Delight from Turkey, by one of the P. and O. steamers; and I'd bring them up to the waxwork. Annabel and I both love children."

"And I hope to my heart you may have some of your own to bless you!" rejoined Mr. Greatorex with unaccountable emotion. "To bless you when they are young ; to bless you when they—when they—shall be grown. God grant you may never have cause to weep for them in tears of blood ! Many of earth's sorrows are hard to bear, but that is the weightiest that Heaven can inflict upon us."

Roland stared a little. The thing seemed nearly as incomprehensible to his view of social life, as that he should have to weep for some defect in the moon.

" We'd bring them up in the best way, Mr. Greatorex," was the simple answer. " Annabel would, you may be sure, and I'd try to. I don't think I got brought up in the best way myself : there was too much scuffling and scrambling. Mrs. J. once said—I beg your pardon, Annabel."

For Annabel was trying to express to Mr. Greatorex their regret at his son's death. The strange emotion that had shaken him she knew must be felt for Bede.

" We are both of us very sorry, sir, for him and for you," she said.

" My dear, you need not be," spoke Mr. Greatorex, in a low, sad tone. " His life had grown weary ; and death, to him, must have been like a welcome rest at the close of day. A little sooner, a little later—what does it matter ?"

"And for the muffs of doctors not to be able to cure him! Mr. Greatorex, when I remember him, and Vincent Yorke, and Hamish Channing, my respect for the medical profession does not go up. Halloa! who's this?" broke off Roland.

Philip was coming in with a cloud of surprise on his face, while a rustle as of extensive petticoats might be heard in his rear. He addressed his master with deprecation, conscious of something to tell that might not be very agreeable.

"It is Mrs. Bede Greatorex, sir."

"Who?" hurriedly exclaimed Mr. Greatorex.

"Mr. Bede's widow, sir. She has arrived with a French maid and a cab full of boxes."

No need to reiterate the news, for Mrs. Bede stood in view. Mr. Greatorex seized his servant by the coat like one in alarm, and gave a private order.

"Keep the cab. Don't unload the boxes. Mrs. Bede Greatorex will not remain here."

Mrs. Bede Greatorex, a widow of a month, was not less fashionable in appearance than when she was a wife. Rather more so, of the two. Her dress of rich silk and crape was a model for the mode books, her hair was wonderful to behold. A small bob of something white peeped out atop of the chignon; looking close, it might be discovered to be an inch of quilled net: and its wearer called it a widow's cap with all the brass in life.

She held out her hand to Mr. Greatorex, but he seemed not to see it. That his resentment against this woman was one of bitterness, could not be mistaken. Mrs. Bede did not appear to notice the coldness of the greeting. Brushing past Annabel, she cast a rather contemptuous look towards her, and said some slighting words.

"What! are *you* here again? I thought the house was rid of you."

"This is my wife; Lady Yorke," spoke Roland in as haughty a tone as it was possible for him to assume. "Don't forget it, if you please, Mrs. Bede Greatorex."

She looked from one to the other of them. That Roland had succeeded to the family honours, she knew, but she had not heard of his marriage. The poor young governess, whom she had put upon and made unhappy, Lady Yorke! A moment's pause: Mrs. Bede's manner changed as if by magic, and she kissed Annabel on both cheeks, French fashion. Nobody knew better than she on which side her bread was buttered.

"Ah, dear me, it's fine to be you, Annabel! What changes since we last met. You a wife, and I a widow."

Mr. Greatorex took an impatient step forward, as if to speed her departure. She turned to him, speaking of her husband.

"I think Bede might have got well if he would. I used to tell him so. The doctors made an examination afterwards, and found, as you have heard, that there was no specific disease whatever. He wasted away; wasted and wasted; it was like as though there were a consuming fire ever within him, burning him away to death."

"My goodness!" cried Roland. "Poor Bede."

"It was most unsatisfactory: I never saw anything like it in my life before," tartly retorted Mrs. Bede, for her husband's death had not pleased her, and she resented it openly. Not for the loss or love of him, but for the loss of his means. "I think he might have got well had he struggled for it. If you'll believe me, only the day before he died, he went out in a carriage to the post-office, that he might post a letter himself to Sir Thomas Kene."

No one answered her, or made any comment.

“Is my old room ready for me?”

Mr. Greatorex, to whom the question was more particularly put, motioned her towards the door, and moved thither himself. “I wish to speak with you in private for a minute,” he said. “Pardon me, Sir Roland, I will be back directly.”

That Mrs. Bede Greatorex had come to take the house by storm, hoping thereby to resume her late footing in it, Mr. Greatorex knew just as well as she. His letter to her, delivered by George Winter, was unmistakably plain; and he did wonder at the hardihood which had brought her hither, after its receipt.

“You cannot have misunderstood my communication,” he said to her as they turned into the room that had once been her boudoir. “I must beg to refer you to it. This house can never shelter you again.”

“But it must,” she answered.

“Never again; never again.”

“At least, I must stay here for some days, until I can decide where my residence shall be,” she persisted, her voice taking the unpleasant shriek that it always took in anger. “You can’t deny me that.”

Mr. Greatorex raised his hand as if to waive off the argument and the words.

" Philip shall see you to an hotel, if you feel incompetent to drive to one with your maid," he said, slightly sarcastic.   " But, under my roof; it once sheltered in happiness my poor son ; you may not remain."

" I was your son's wife," she passionately said.

" I will tell you what you were to him, if you wish.   I don't press it."

" Well ?"

" His curse."

" Thank you."

" His curse before marriage ; his curse after it."

As he stood there, with his face of pain, speaking not in an angry tone, but one mournfully subdued, certain items connected with the past rose up to fill the mind of Mrs. Bede Greatorex.   She was aware then that he knew all ; she had some little shame left in her, and her very brow grew crimson.

" I cannot imagine what you may have heard, or be suspecting," she said, falteringly. " The past is past.   I did nothing very wrong. Nothing but what plenty of other girls do."

" May God forgive you, Louisa Greatorex ; as I know He has forgiven *him*."

It was surging up in her mind like angry waves, that far gone-by time, one event replacing another. During her prolonged visit to this very house as Louisa Joliffe, she had suffered Bede to become passionately attached to her. Suffered ?—it was she who drew him and drew him on. She engaged herself to him privately; a solemn engagement; and Bede acceded to her request that it should be kept secret for a time. She did not like Bede ; she was playing an utterly false part ; she coveted the good income and position that would be hers as his wife, but she rather disliked him. Her motive in demanding that their engagement should be concealed, was a hope that some offer more desirable might turn up. Oh that Bede had suspected it ! He looked for her to be his wife as surely as he looked for Heaven. After her return home from her visit, and John Ollivera was sojourning at Helstonleigh, she played exactly the same game over with him. Drawing him on to love her, and engaging herself to him in private. She liked *him*, but she did not like to have to wait an indefinite number of years, until the young barrister should find himself in a position to marry. Which of the two she would eventually have chosen, was a matter that must remain in uncertainty for ever; most likely (she acknowledged so to herself) Bede and his wealth. Things went on smoothly enough, she corresponding ardently with both of them in secret, until the time of the March assizes —so often told of—and the fatal night when Bede Greatorex came down to Helstonleigh on a mission to his cousin. The contretemps, the almost certainty of discovery, the very probable fear that she should lose both her lovers, nearly drove Louisa out of her senses. That something in connection with it had passed between Bede and his cousin, she knew from Bede's manner that evening at her mother's; how much, she did not dare to ask. The following morning, when the news was brought to her that Mr. Ollivera had destroyed himself, she felt like a guilty woman. Whatever might have been the mystery of the death : whether he had really committed suicide, or whether Bede had shot him in the passion of his hot Spanish blood—and it was impossible but that she should have her latent doubts—*she* was the primary cause; and she knew it, and felt it. Had she gone out and killed him herself, she could not have felt it more. She became aware of another thing—that Bede Greatorex, searching amidst the effects of the dead on the following day, must have found her love-letters : more impassioned letters than she was wont to write to *him*. Bede did not visit her again during his stay at Helstonleigh, and she would not have dared to seek him. Some months later they met by accident in London : were thrown together three or four times. Bede renewed his offer of marriage, and she accepted him at once ; the doubt in her mind, as to the part he might have taken in John Ollivera's death, never having been solved. She conveniently ignored it, for the glowing prospect of an establishment was all in all. But what sort of a wife did she make him ?—how much did Bede, in his chivalric devotion, have to bear ? She alone knew ; she knew it now as she stood there ; and her attempt to carry it off with a high hand to Mr. Greatorex failed signally. If ever the true sense of her sin should be brought home by Heaven to Louisa Greatorex, its weight, as connected with the treatment of her husband, would be well-nigh greater than she could bear. A curse to him before marriage ; a curse to him after : Mr. Greatorex had well said it.

"Am I to starve in future, that you won't give me a home ?" she burst forth, driving other thoughts away from her. "What's two hundred a-year ? How am I to live ?"

"My recommendation to you was, that you should live in Boulogne ; with, or near your mother," Mr. Greatorex answered calmly.

"The two hundred pounds will be amply sufficient for that."

"Two hundred pounds!" she retorted, rudely. "I shall spend that on my dress."

"As you please, of course. It is the sum that will be paid you in quarterly instalments of fifty pounds, as long as I live. At my death, the half of it only would be secured to you. Should you marry again, the payments would altogether cease. All this I stated to you in my letter: I repeat it now. Not another shilling will you receive from me—in life, or after death."

She saw her future; saw it all laid out before her as on a map; and her face took a blank look, betraying mortification and despair. No more ravishing toilettes or French waiting maids; no more costly dinner-givings, or magnificent kettle-drums. Mrs. Bede Greatorex and society must henceforth live tolerably far apart. The home she had so despised, this that she was now being turned from, would be a very palace compared to the lodgings in Boulogne.

"To prolong this interview will not be productive of further result," spoke Mr. Greatorex, taking a step towards the door. "I must beg to remind you that friends are waiting for me."

" And my clothes, that I left here? And the ornaments that were mine?"

" Everything belonging to you has been packed ready for removal. The cases shall be all sent to whatever place you may name."

She turned away without another word. Mr. Greatorex rang the bell. Outside, sitting underneath one of the white statues, near the small conservatory, was the French maid, inwardly railing against the want of politeness of these misérable Anglishe. Trusty Philip had warned her that she need not go up higher.

The cab drove away with them, and Mr. Greatorex returned to the dining-room with a relieved heart.

" She is done with at last, thank Heaven! Let us have tea together, Roland," he added, with a hearty smile. " Lady Yorke will take off her bonnet, and make it for us; as she did when she was my little friend Annabel Channing."

⁂   ⁂   ⁂   ⁂   ⁂

Copy of the letter received by Judge Kene from Bede Greatorex.

" As you know so much, Sir Thomas, I owe it to you and to myself to afford some further explanation. You have shown your-

20—2

self a true friend : add to the obligation, by imparting the details I now write to Henry William Ollivera.

"When I was despatched to Helstonleigh on that fatal mission, I was engaged to be married to Louisa Joliffe, and loved her passionately. The engagement had existed several months, but it was at her request kept a secret to ourselves. After delivering the message and business I was charged with to John, we sat on, in his room, talking of indifferent matters. I said that I should spend the evening with the Joliffes : John laughed a little, and said perhaps he should. One word led to another, and at last he told me, premising it must be in confidence, that he was engaged to Louisa. I thought he was joking ; my answer annoyed him ; and he went on to say things about Louisa's love for him and their future marriage that nearly drove me wild. What, I hardly know now. It seemed to me that he had treacherously stepped in to strive to take my bride from me, to win her for himself, my one little ewe lamb. We recriminated on each other : she had deceived us both, but neither of us suspected it then : and we felt something like rival tiger cats ; at least I know I did. Whenever my Spanish blood got up I was a

Mr. Bede Greatorex. It was my face he saw, Kene ; no other. All through these years he has watched my misery ; and in his great compassion for what he knew my sufferings must be, has been silently lightening life to me where he could. But, to go back to the time.

"I should think we gazed at each other for the space of half a minute, the man on the stairs and I : the fright of seeing some one there nearly paralysed me ; and then I went in again and shut the door. It was perhaps the sight of him that caused me to attempt to throw the suspicion off myself : certainly I had not thought of it before. I put the pistol on the carpet by the chair, as if it had fallen from John's right hand ; and next, looking about on the table, I found the unfinished letter, and added the lines you know of. I seemed to be doing it in a dream ; that it was not myself but somebody else, and all in a desperate hurry, for I grew afraid of stopping. Then it occurred to me to put out the lamp ; I don't know why ; and, upon that, I went out resolutely, for I did not like the dark. Luck seemed to be against me. As I opened the door this second time, some young man (not the first) was passing by. Instinct caused me to turn round and make believe to be speaking to John. What words I really said, I should never have remembered but for hearing the young man, Alfred Jones, repeat them at the coroner's inquest. They served me more than I thought : for Alfred Jones unconsciously took up the natural supposition that John was also speaking to me ; this version went forth to the public, and it was assumed that what happened, happened after my departure. There's no doubt that it was the chief element in throwing suspicion off me. He showed me out of the house, and thenceforward I had to try and act the part of an innocent man. I went to the Star and Garter and drank some brandy-and-water ; I went thence to Mrs. Joliffe's : how I did it all, with that horrible thing upon me, I have never known. I said a few cautious words to Louisa, and by her answers, I felt sure that John's boast had been (at least in part) a vain one. As I returned up High Street, some tradesman was standing just within his side-door. He did not know I saw him. Halting, I looked at John Ollivera's windows, just opposite, and said something to the effect that John must have gone to bed—all for the man to hear me. Just afterwards I met you, Kene,—do you remember it ? You were going to call on John, but I said he had gone

madman—as you may remember, Kene, for you
saw me so once or twice in earlier days—I
was nothing else that wicked evening. At
some taunt of his, or it sounded like one to
me, I took up the pistol, that lay on the
table underneath my hand, and fired it at
him. Before Heaven, where I shall so soon
stand, I declare that I had no deliberate intention of killing him. I did not know
whether the pistol was loaded or not. I
do not even think I knew what I was doing,
or that I had caught up the pistol : in my
mad rage I was conscious of nothing. The
shot killed him instantaneously, even in the
midst of his cry. I cried out too—with
horror at what I had done ; my passion faded,
and I stood still as he was. Before I crossed
the step or two to his succour, I saw that he
was dead. How horribly I have repented
since that I did not fling open the door and
call out for assistance, none, save myself, can
know. Self-preservation lies instinctively
within us all, and I suppose that stopped me.
Oh, the false coward that I have since ever
called myself !—the years of concealment and
misery it would have saved ! All I thought
of then, was—to get away. A short while I
listened, but no sound told that any one had
been within earshot; I softly opened the door to

escape, putting out my head first to reconnoitre ; and—found myself nearly face to face with a man. He stood on the stairs in an attitude of listening, and our eyes met in the gas-light. I never forgot his ; they seemed to shine out from a mass of black hair ; those same eyes afterwards puzzled my memory for years. When the eyes of my subsequent clerk, Mr. Brown, had used to strike some unpleasant chord on my memory, but what I could not fathom, I never connected them with those other eyes ; for Brown had put off his disguise then, and looked entirely another person. Ah, Kene ! don't you see the obligation I lie under to this man, George Winter ? Not at that moment did he know I had committed murder, but in a short period of time, as soon as the newspapers supplied details of the night's doings, he could but become aware of it. Had a doubt remained on his mind, when he entered our office and knew me for Bede Greatorex, the thing must have been made clear to him as daylight. To shield me he has remained under a cloud himself : I hope my father will reward him. Even when he was giving his evidence before you and the rest, he told a lie to save me. For he said that when he saw the face at the door, it was *after* the departure of to bed and the people of the house, too, I supposed, as there was no light to be seen. I shrunk from the discovery, and would fain have put it off for ever. What a night that was for me! As I had stirred the tea at Mrs. Joliffe's, as I stirred the brandy-and-water at the hotel, John's face seemed to be in the liquid, staring up at me. In the dark of the bed-room, after the candle had burnt out, I saw him in his chair, just as I had left him. I had not dared to ask for a night-light, lest it might excite suspicion: how could I answer for it that the hotel would not get to learn I was not in the habit of burning one?

"You know the rest: the discovery and the inquest that followed. Did I act my part well, Kene? I suppose so, by the result. That day—the first—you were with me when we examined John's desk: it was advised that I should look over his letters for any clue that perhaps they might show to the motive of his self-inflicted death. The large bundle of letters, Kene, came I found from Louisa Joliffe, and poor John's was no vain boast: she had been all to him that she had professed to be to me, and a traitor to both.

"Why did I marry her, you will naturally ask. Ah, why! why! Because my love for her fooled me into it: because, if you will, I was mad. When we met again, months afterwards, the passion that I thought I had killed within me, rose up with ten-fold force, and I yielded to it. To do so was not much less sinful (looking at it as I look now) than the other and greater crime. I saw it even as I stood with her before the altar, I saw it afterwards clearer and clearer. But I loved her even in spite of my better judgment; I love her even yet: and I have striven to do my duty by her in all indulgence, to shield her from the cares of the world.

"And there's my life's history. Oh, Kene, if I have been more sinful than other men, my merciful God knows what my expiation has been. Can you even faintly picture it to yourself? From a few minutes after the breath went out of poor John's body, my punishment set in. It was only fear just at first; it was the bitterest remorse afterwards that ever made a wreck of mortal man. I am not a murderer by nature, and John and I were dear friends. My days have been one long, wearing penance: regret for him and his shortened life, dread of my crime's discovery; one or the other filling every moment: remorse and repentance, repentance and remorse: and that it has been so is owing to Heaven's mercy. Not an hour of the day or night, but I would gladly have given up my own life to restore his. After the first confused horror had passed, I should have declared the truth at the time but for my mother's sake : in her state of health it would have killed her. When she died, the time had gone by for it : I had my father and my wife to consider later, and remained perforce silent. My father has thought my bodily health failed : in one sense so it did, for I have been wasting away from the first, dying slowly inch by inch.

"And that's all, Kene. When you shall have heard news of my death—it will be with you very close upon this letter—disclose the whole to Henry William Ollivera. With regard to my father, I leave the matter to you. If he in the slightest degree suspects me—and I can but think he must, after Winter's confession, and from the easy acquiescence he gave to my coming on the Continent for an indefinite period—then tell him the whole. Heaven bless you all, and grant you the peace that can spring alone of Jesus Christ's atonement ! I have dared to think it mine for some little time now.

"BEDE GREATOREX."

When the tidings of Bede's death reached

him, Sir Thomas Kene went out to seek an interview with Mr. Ollivera. The clergyman read the letter, and bent his head in prolonged silence.

"After all, I suppose John's grave will have to remain undisturbed," spoke the Judge. "Winter cleared his memory."

"Yes ; better so, perhaps," was the slow, thoughtful reply. "If I had never before been thankful that I read the burial service over him, I should be so now. You see, I was right, Kene. God be merciful to us all, for we are miserable sinners !"

THE END.

BILLING, PRINTER, GUILDFORD.

www.ingramcontent.com/pod-product-compliance
Lightning Source LLC
Chambersburg PA
CBHW031025120726
47905CB00007B/2043